HIS BEAUTY

Also by Sofia Tate

Breathless for Him
Devoted to Him
Forever with Him
Crazy for Him (novella)

HIS BEAUTY

Sofia Tate

**FOREVER
YOURS**

New York   Boston

Copyright © 2018 by Sofia Tate
Excerpt from *Her Beast* copyright © 2018 by Sofia Tate
Cover design by Elizabeth Turner Stokes
Cover copyright © 2018 by Hachette Book Group, Inc.
Hachette Book Group supports the right to free expression and the value of copyright. The purpose of copyright is to encourage writers and artists to produce the creative works that enrich our culture.

The scanning, uploading, and distribution of this book without permission is a theft of the author's intellectual property. If you would like permission to use material from the book (other than for review purposes), please contact permissions@hbgusa.com. Thank you for your support of the author's rights.

Forever Yours
Hachette Book Group
1290 Avenue of the Americas
New York, NY 10104
forever-romance.com
twitter.com/foreverromance

First ebook and print on demand edition: May 2018

Forever Yours is an imprint of Grand Central Publishing. The Forever Yours name and logo are trademarks of Hachette Book Group, Inc.

The publisher is not responsible for websites (or their content) that are not owned by the publisher.

The Hachette Speakers Bureau provides a wide range of authors for speaking events. To find out more, go to www.hachettespeakersbureau.com or call (866) 376-6591.

ISBN 978-1-4555-6581-8 (ebook edition)
ISBN 978-1-5387-1330-3 (print on demand edition)

For my Catskills lovelies
Antonia, Meabh, and Sadhbh at
The Windham Spa
Cordelia at Ze Windham Wine Bar and
Roxanne at my local post office
Thank you for your friendship, making me
laugh when I needed it most, and being there
for me when I was at my lowest.
Love, S. xoxo

HIS BEAUTY

HIS BEAUTY

Chapter One

The ten-year-old with the gap teeth and blond pigtails stares back at me.

"Meeley," she insists.

"It's not Meeley, Olenka. It's Miley."

As much as I dislike talking about pop singers with my second graders, I believe it's my duty as a teacher of English as a Second Language to at least correct my students' pronunciation.

"Yes, Miss Lily. I know. Meeley Cyrus. She played Hannah Dakota."

As well as teach her the correct state. "It's Hannah Montana, which is right next to North Dakota."

"Who is North Dakota?" she asks with a confused look crossing her face.

"It's a state, stupid," Ramon, a skinny boy with Harry Potter-like glasses, offers in reply.

Head-desk.

I turn to Ramon. "Please read Class Rule number 2 out loud so everyone can hear."

His face turns beet red, swallowing before he begins. "We do not call each other bad names."

"Thank you, Ramon. Now please apologize to Olenka."

He pivots in his chair to her. "I'm sorry, Olenka."

She nods shyly. "Okay, Ramon."

Thankfully, at that exact moment, the PA system crackles to life. The steady voice of Cottage Grove School's principal, Mr. Henry Palmer, comes over the system with the final announcements for the day.

"Good afternoon, boys and girls. I hope you all had a productive day of learning. I have no announcements, just to wish you a lovely holiday. I look forward to seeing all of you in the New Year."

The sound of papers shuffling over the PA echoes into the room.

"Actually, I do have one announcement. Miss Lily Moore, please come to my office after the final bell." The PA system shuts off with a squeak.

I'm sure it's nothing.

My ten ESL students instantly emit a Pavlovian response of "Oooh! You're in trouble!"

I sigh to myself. *Great.*

"I'm sure it's nothing. Now, you know the drill. Pack up your bags, get your jackets, chairs on top of your desks, and quietly line up at the door single file."

Per their usual daily routine they follow my instructions, without the quiet component.

Once I lead the students outside and ensure they're safe with their parents or parent-approved minders, I take a deep breath and head back inside the one-story brick building and down the hallway to the principal's office. I wait in the outer room for the okay from his secretary, looking out the window at the snow-covered Catskill Mountains across the Hudson River. An intercom buzzes, indicating I'm allowed to enter.

Dressed in his usual tweed jacket with a button-down shirt and tie and tortoise-shell glasses, Mr. Palmer resembles a college professor more than a grammar school principal. He is mild-mannered and kind, and even chivalrous, rising to his feet when I walk in.

"Miss Moore, please," he says, gesturing to the chair in front of his desk.

"Thank you," I reply with a nod, placing my hands folded together in my lap, sitting up straight to give him my full attention.

I look directly at my boss, who smiles at me sheepishly, then stretches his arms out on top of his desk, folding his hands together like mine are, but then he bounces them up and down on the oak wood, clearing his throat.

Oh, shit. This isn't good news.

"Miss Moore, I hope you know how much I appreciate your work here. I never receive anything but rave reviews from the other teachers, your students, and their parents."

I give him a small smile. "Thank you, sir."

He sighs audibly.

Please, just pull off the damn Band-Aid and get this over with.

"I heard from the school board today. Apparently, they hired an efficiency expert and she concluded that a separate ESL class is not cost feasible for the district."

"What does that mean?"

"It means that after the Christmas break, you won't have your own classroom anymore."

My mouth drops; my hands clench together now even more tightly. "But what about the students? They need ESL. You can't put them into the mainstream classes. Many of them have serious issues, and not just the lack of English proficiency. Some of them barely say a word in class, and many have never even been in a classroom setting before—"

Mr. Palmer holds up his palms to me, effectively telling me to stop talking. "I know. Believe me, I repeated those same sentiments to the board members, but because of the size of our district, money comes before the needs of the students."

I swallow before asking the question, dreading the answer. "So, what happens to me?"

He gives me a conciliatory smile. "Well, the good news is that you'll still be teaching. Tutoring, really. The board approved funds for after-school ESL tutoring sessions twice a week."

"Twice a week?" I screech. "There's no way that's enough time with them!"

Shocked at my outburst, my face grows red in embarrassment. "Mr. Palmer, I'm so sorry. I didn't mean for it to come out like that."

He shakes his head at me. "Please, no need for an apology. I actually admire your passion for your students and their learning. But I need to know if you're interested in still continuing with them."

I practically jump up in my seat. "Yes, of course."

"Silly question. I knew you would say that, but I'm glad to hear it just the same. You'll start the tutoring after Christmas break. Of course, your pay will be half of what you earn now."

Of course.

"Is there anything else, sir?"

"No, that's all for now. I'm so sorry about this. I truly am."

I look at my principal's face, his mouth downturned, his eyes soft and sympathetic, and I believe him.

I rise from the chair. "Thank you, Mr. Palmer. I appreciate your kindness in this situation."

He follows, coming to his feet and extending his hand to me. "Miss Moore, if there's anything you need, do let me know. I hope you have a lovely holiday with your family."

Yes, Merry fucking Christmas to me.

I slap on a grin and nod. "I wish you the same."

I walk out of my boss's office in a fog. If anyone addresses me, I don't hear them. I reach my classroom and walk straight to my desk chair, the one I've sat in for two years, and slump my body down into it. I glance around the room at the colorful posters I've put up; the maps of the countries where my students were born, with push pins marking their hometowns; their work stapled to various bulletin boards, gold stars contrasting against the lined notebook paper. I want to cry so much, but I can't afford to.

I reach for my purse, rummaging around in it for my phone. I need to call Reed. I need to hear my boyfriend tell me everything will be fine and it'll all work out the way it's supposed to.

I listen as the phone rings once, twice…then goes straight to voicemail.

Damn it.

I shake my head and throw my cell back into my purse. I grab my tote bag, locking my classroom behind me. I wrap my wool scarf tighter around my neck as a cold breeze hits my face the second I step outside.

A light dusting of snow covers the hood of my dark blue Volvo. I shove the key in the lock, hip-checking the driver's side door of my baby, which I inherited from my mom six years ago.

Once I secure myself with the seat belt I greet my Swedish car lovingly, petting the steering wheel. "Hello, Ingrid. You'll get me home safely today, *ja?* Because I've had a crap day and I can't deal with any more shit right now. I'd be really grateful. 'kay, thanks."

I turn the key and Ingrid comes to life, bless her. Backing out of my assigned space, I drive out of the staff parking lot, turning west for my alma mater.

Like other upstate New York colleges such as Ithaca and Skidmore, Ashby College is a liberal arts college known for its small class sizes and professors who challenge and inspire. Located on the edge of Hudson, a town with bustling art galleries, antique stores, and bistros, it was my first choice when I was applying to college. It helped that I lived across the river in Catskill, so I could commute to campus.

But with all of my student loan debts, living on half my current pay isn't an option. I need to find a second job.

I love Ashby's campus. It's spread out across rolling green lawns, and there are oak trees everywhere, the buildings all low and red brick. My favorite feature is the collection of sculptures by Ashby grads who have become famous artists in their own right.

I pull into the visitor parking lot, give Ingrid another hip-check when I shut the door, then make my way toward the admin building. I walk up the stairs, turning right for the career services office. I greet the staff with a smile, masking my desperation.

An older woman occupying the seat at the reception desk glances at me curiously. "Looking for a job, sweetie?"

"Just something part-time. Could I…?" I ask, gesturing toward the computers for students' use.

"Of course. Nice and quiet today, so take as long as you need."

"Thanks."

I plant myself in front of one of the monitors, dropping my purse to the floor. I use my old Ashby user ID and password, which are still valid, thank God. I click on the link for part-time jobs and begin scanning the listings. There are various positions—babysitting, snow shoveling, baristas at a local café.

I sigh in frustration.

None of them interest me until one catches my eye.

"Part-time house cleaner wanted for single occupant home. 2 days a week. Light cleaning. No cooking. No laundry. Excellent compensation."

The "excellent compensation" line grabs my attention. There is no phone number listed, only an email address with the name "SEstate." The name disconcerts me, but I don't care. It could be some old money family in Hudson with a mansion overlooking the river that wants someone to wax their floors like Cinderfuck-ingrella. But now…desperate times, desperate measures.

I pull out my thumb drive from my purse and connect it to the computer's tower. I knock out a quick cover letter, attaching my résumé from the drive, and hit send. Logging out, I thank the receptionist and head for the exit, pulling my wool hat tighter over my head and turning up the collar on my coat to face the bitter cold outside.

* * *

I pull into the driveway of the two-story A-frame house I call home. With its wraparound front deck, two large front windows, and three small windows on the second floor lined with flower boxes—all of it covered in a light coating of snow—the entire structure could have been airlifted straight from the Swiss Alps.

And I hate it. It's too cute, too sweet. Too perfect.

But it's what came with the package when I met Reed Shepard—of the Shepards of Saratoga Springs—at a mixer freshman year, so I had to swallow the fact that he lived in a house straight out of *Heidi*.

We live in a section of Cottage Grove known as Cottage Grove Hills. It was founded back in the 1920s by a group of families from the Capitol Region of Albany who wanted a place in the country. Their blood runs blue; their names are permanently featured in every annual edition of the *Social Register*.

I turn off Ingrid's engine and pat the steering wheel, wishing her good night.

I get out of the car and shake my head at the sight of Reed's BMW sedan covered in its protective tarp that he had custom made for it. He always covers it during inclement weather, which is so ridiculous since the weather in the Catskills is inclement ninety-nine percent of the winter season. The Shepards overlooked one important component of the house when they had it built—the garage—but I figure that was on purpose so they could show off their various luxury automobiles.

I stomp my feet on the mat outside the door to shake off any residual snow. "I'm home," I shout when I walk through the door.

"Study," I hear Reed reply in return.

I drop my bag on the sofa in the living room and make my way to the book-paneled room where Reed is sitting at his desk, his eyes fixed on the computer screen in front of him.

Dressed in a light blue long-sleeved polo shirt and his Ashby sweats, he doesn't acknowledge my entrance.

I walk over to him and kiss the top of his head. "How are you?"

"Stressed," he replies curtly.

I glance at his desk, where open copies of science textbooks are strewn about. "What's going on?"

"Hopkins told me the new department chair is going to observe me next week in my Computer Science 101 class. If I do well, she's going to recommend me for a full-time position, so I have to knock the lesson plan out of the park."

"Have you met the new chair yet?"

"No, but I've heard mixed things about her, which doesn't help."

Reed is an adjunct computer science professor at Ashby, teaching mostly the 101 level courses to incoming freshmen as part of their prereqs. I never mention to him that he probably won't be promoted since he doesn't have a PhD. As loving and caring as he is, Reed tends to live in his blue-blooded world, where the right name and money can buy anything. In my family, the blood doesn't run blue, but its collar does.

This is why I clear my throat before I share my news with him. "Honey, I need to tell you something."

He runs his hands through his hair. "Can it wait?"

"They're taking my classroom away from me."

His head whips around, his eyes widened in shock. "Why?"

"The school board decided to cut the ESL program, so I'll only be a tutor in the after-school program when the holiday break is over, which means my pay will be cut in half and I'll need to get a second job."

"When did you find out?"

"Today. Palmer called me into his office after class." I glance over and point to his cell sitting on the desk next to his computer. "You would've known all this if you'd answered your phone when I called you about two hours ago."

He pauses and picks up his phone to check the screen. "Fuck."

Reed rises from his chair and studies my face carefully, then shakes his head, running his hands through his hair. "I'm so sorry, babe. I'm really worried about the observation, the new department chair…"

I step closer to him, folding him into my arms "It's okay, honey. I know. You've been working so hard trying to prove yourself to the faculty that you forget about everything else."

"You're right. So, this means you probably won't be home until after five once you start tutoring?"

I pull back from him, his segue into another topic completely catching me off guard. "Probably, but what does that have to do with anything?"

"I always loved coming home from class, knowing you'd be waiting for me."

I can't help but smile at the memories his comment conjures. "I know. Remember that lacy black number I got from Victoria's—"

"I loved walking in and smelling what you cooked for dinner." *He's kidding, right?*

"I'm sorry, but the last time I checked, we live in a town called Cottage Grove Hills, not Stepford."

He bites his lower lip. "Damn it. Sorry, Lil. I know I'm being such a shit. I promise once this observation is over, I'll be the sweet, caring guy you fell in love with. But I just have to get this done, okay?"

I grin at his reply. "I know you will. I was thinking for dinner—"

He releases his hold on me and sits back down at his desk. "Yeah, whatever you want, babe. Doesn't matter to me. I just need to get this done."

I shut my eyes as my shoulders turn inward into my chest, almost as if they're forming a protective shell around me. I place my hand on my belly to settle myself. The hollow pit where my stomach used to be. Goose bumps pop up all over my arms from his less than warm reaction to my announcement.

No 'it'll be okay,' no 'we'll get through this together.'
He's never been like this before.
It's fine. It's fine. I know the reason. He's stressed. He loves me. He's only like this because he loves his job and wants to be hired for a full-time position.

I slowly retreat from the room, biting my lips together. I take slow, deep breaths. I pick up my purse and tote bag in the living room.

A pair of strong arms encircles my waist, pulling me toward a warm body.

Reed holds me tightly, his warm breath in my right ear. "I'm really sorry, babe. I promise I'll make it up to you."

I shut my eyes, placing my hands over his. "I know you are, Reed. It's okay."

He places a soft kiss on my neck before releasing me from his grip. I turn to see him walk back into the study.

When I reach the bedroom, I drop my bags to the floor. Kicking off my shoes, I fall back onto the bed, fusing my eyes shut. I clench my lips together, taking deep breaths to calm myself.

But only one place truly brings me the calm I need.

Jumping off the bed, I sling my purse over my shoulder. I yank open the bottom drawer of my desk, pulling out the used Nikon that I bought on eBay and drop it into the bottom of my bag.

I don't even bother telling Reed I'm leaving. I doubt he'd even notice. I give Ingrid a nudge to open the driver's door and pull out of the driveway, heading back to campus and the one place that gives me comfort and sanctuary when I need it most.

* * *

So beautiful.

I sit on my favorite bench in my oasis, a few feet from the one object in this world that brings me peace and always lifts my spirits. The sun beams down on me, providing much-needed warmth in the cold weather.

The sculpture was here when I started as an undergrad, and it never ages for me; I find something new to discover about it every time I come here. The moment I saw it on the first day of Ashby College freshman orientation, I stood paralyzed. Our tour guide was discussing meal plans at the time, if I recall correctly, but I zoned her out and focused on them: *The Lovers*. The subject of the sculpture.

Cast in deep bronze, a woman is standing directly in front of a man, her hair cascading down her back, the hem of her dress flowing around her calves, her voluptuous chest pressing into him. The man's forehead leans against the woman's; his arms are wound tightly around her waist. While she is dressed, he is completely naked, his legs hard and muscled, his backside firm and strong.

The most striking feature of the sculpture is what draws me back to this place again and again. The woman is holding his face between her hands, cupping it as if it were the most precious thing in the world. To me, she is comforting him, and I only wish I knew why.

I pull out my Nikon and begin clicking away from my seat. A dusting of snow provides a contrast between the blinding white and the dark stone as I focus the lens so it can capture the lovers' faces as closely as possible. I used to take the pictures with my phone, but after a while I realized I wanted to take pictures with better color and focus.

Once I finish, I take a deep breath and put the camera away, leaning back on the bench. But then something beckons me to rise up and walk over to the small metal plate fitted to the right side of the sculpture. I know what's written there by heart, even though it's only four words. It simply reads:

The Lovers
  Grayson Shaw

All I know about Grayson Shaw is what I've discovered over the years on the Internet. From a wealthy local family, he is an alumnus of Ashby, although I've never found his name listed in any yearbook. He's had exhibits of his work all over the world, but never attends any of them. I don't even know how old he is, but I almost feel closer to him than I do to Reed, my college sweetheart, the man I plan to marry someday.

I stare at the lovers again.

Do you need comfort, Grayson Shaw? Is that what you need, what you want more than anything? Why are you so broken?

The sound of my cell phone ringing rouses me from my thoughts.

I rush over to the bench and rummage through my purse. It's a number I don't recognize.

"Hello?"

"Is this Lily Moore?" an older woman's voice asks.

"Yes, it is."

"You responded to an ad about becoming a cleaning woman."

My shoulders drop in relief as my heart begins to race. "Yes, that was me."

"Could you come in tomorrow for an interview?"

I pump my left fist with excitement while holding the phone in my right. "Of course. I'm available any time after 3 p.m."

"3:30 then? Ask for Emilia Mitchell. Let me give you directions."

I dig around in my purse for a pen and my notepad, jotting

them down. I hang up the phone, shouting "Yes!" to myself. I sling my purse over my shoulder, glancing over once more at the sculpture.

I smile at the lovers, my heart full of hope, knowing this makes another moment when they've been a comfort for me when I needed them most. "Wish me luck, Grayson Shaw."

Chapter Two

*U*gh.

I stare at the discarded clothes on my bed.

The last interview I had was for my teaching job two years ago. What the hell do I wear to interview for a job cleaning someone's house?

Oh, fuck it. As long as they don't expect me to show up in a Chanel suit, I'll probably be fine.

I pick up the black twin sweater set I got on sale and pair it with my go-to black tweed pencil skirt. Slipping into my black work pumps, I give myself a once-over in my full-length mirror.

Not bad. It'll have to do.

I rush downstairs and quickly print out two copies of my résumé from the desktop computer I share with Reed in our study, then grab a manila envelope from the desk so I don't wrinkle them.

Shoving the envelope into my tote bag, I glance up at the wall covered with family photos of Reed with his parents at his childhood home. All three of them are dressed impeccably, Reed and his father in tailored suits and his mother in a cream dress with her ever-present pearls looped around her neck.

I take a deep breath, already predicting what their reaction will be when they find out that their son's girlfriend might be accepting a job as a cleaning lady.

As nice as they are to my face, I know if pressed, Reed's parents would admit they think I'm all wrong for their son, the heir to the Shepard fortune. I know it kills them that Reed wasn't accepted at any Ivy League college, not even Cornell, where his father and grandfather had attended. He'd fooled around too much at boarding school, and got kicked out of one and only accepted into another because his parents made a huge donation to restore the school's library.

They won't be pleased to be sure, knowing the woman their son is dating is a cleaning lady, but I can take it.

My mom raised me all by herself, taking odd jobs to get through nursing school, watching every penny she made. But she did it, pride be damned.

They'll just have to deal with it because I am my mother's daughter.

* * *

"Come on, Ingrid. You can do it, sweetie."

In fear of wiping out from black ice, I slowly drive up a steep hill a few miles out of town before making a right onto a road lined on either side with majestic oak trees. Out of nowhere a tall stone wall appears, obscuring whatever sits on the other side of it.

I glance briefly at the directions on my phone. Sure enough, just as Emilia described, sections of the wall are separated and allow for a solid black metal gate. The gate is topped by the letter "S" welded into a curlicue font.

A small security camera sits affixed to the left side of the wall, pointing down at me. An intercom speaker is embedded into the stone. I roll down the window, looking straight into the camera.

I'm about to open my mouth to yell out to the open air, not knowing where to direct my voice, but a female voice stops me.

"Miss Moore, please drive through the gates and park to the side of the house where you see my car. I'll meet you out front."

I hear a whirring sound and turn my head to see the gate opening slowly. I drive Ingrid through, onto a long road extending ahead of me. Open acres of parkland expand on both sides of the driveway.

Continuing down the driveway, I suddenly gasp at the sight in front of me, pressing hard on the brakes until they screech, bringing the car to a full stop.

A mansion fronted by two tall columns stands in a cul-de-sac at the end of the pebbled road. Vines wind up and down its concrete exterior, and its surface is full of cracks. I can tell it once probably had a more majestic appearance, but now it looks as if the owners have simply given up on it.

I pull up to the house. An older woman—dressed in a white cotton button-down shirt and loose grey silk pants, her silver hair cut pixie style and a pair of glasses hanging around her neck on a jeweled chain—waves to me, then gestures to the side of the house where an older dark brown Mercedes sedan is parked. I guide Ingrid over and park.

I shut the door as firmly and as quietly as I can and head toward the woman.

I take notice of a fountain centered in front of the house, also dilapidated, dry as a bone except for the dirty rainwater that's collected in it. In the center sits a sculpture also showing its age, covered in moss and cracks, of a young woman with long flowing hair, bent over holding a bucket in her hands as if she's collecting water.

"Hello. I'm Emilia Mitchell, but you can call me Emilia. We're not very formal here. Thank you for coming," the woman says, extending her hand.

I take her hand in mine. "I'm Lily Moore. Thank you for your call."

"Do come in." She turns and opens the tall black door behind her.

I step through the doorway into the foyer, where a huge crystal chandelier hangs from a high ceiling. Several of its bulbs are unlit. There is a long staircase to the left, leading up to the second floor, its carpet worn. The black-and-white marble-tiled floor looks like a checkerboard. There are two sets of closed double doors to my left and right.

I notice a line of framed sketches hung along the walls as I follow Emilia to the back of the house, one of which catches my eye as I walk by it. I stop to observe it up close because it looks so familiar.

I shake my head. *No, it couldn't be. An artist must live here, that's all.*

Continuing down the hall, I spot a living room with several threadbare couches scattered about. Several sets of French doors open to the back of the house.

We turn to the left and enter a small hallway that leads to a huge chef's kitchen—there are two stoves, and pots and pans hang from hooks above a long marble island with a wood base. A small breakfast nook in the far corner holds a round table and four chairs.

Emilia signals to the table. "Please. Coffee? Tea?"

The idea of drinking something cool right now tempts my dry throat. "May I have some water?"

"Certainly. Have a seat."

I sit down in one of the chairs at the table, which is decorated with a ceramic bowl holding a handful of ripe lemons. A folded piece of paper, notepad, and pen lie next to it.

Emilia comes back to the table and hands me a glass of cool water. I take two deep swallows, placing the glass on the table.

I start to pull out the fresh copies of my résumé from the manila envelope but the woman waves her hand at me. "No need, dear. I have a copy right here. But thank you."

"Of course." I tuck the envelope back into my bag, then fold my hands in my lap, ready for her questions.

She places her glasses on the bridge of her nose, pulling the folded paper toward her and opening it. "Thank you for replying so quickly. Our maid broke her leg last week falling down the stairs and unfortunately will be out until it heals. Poor thing was carrying the vacuum and tripped."

I nod at the information, nervous for the answer to the question I'm about to ask. "May I ask you something?"

She nods her head. "Go ahead."

"Exactly how much of the house am I expected to clean? The house is…"

"Rather large?" she offers.

My shoulders drop in relief from her understanding. "Yes."

"The owner prefers that only the kitchen, guest bathroom, foyer, and upstairs hallway are maintained. The rest of the rooms are not your responsibility."

"I see. And it's only for two days a week?"

"Yes. You can start at ten in the morning, and leave any time after you've finished for the day."

This keeps sounding better and better. But it's just too good to be true.

"May I ask what the exact salary is?"

She pulls the notepad to her and writes on it. When she pushes the paper toward me, I nearly jump out of the chair in a mixture of shock and pure joy from the number she's written down.

"Would that work for you?"

Ummm, hell yes.

"It would. Very much."

"Do you need to give your other job two weeks' notice, or can you start immediately?"

"I can start whenever you need me."

"Well, then, if you want the job, it's yours."

I sit back in my chair, pursing my lips together. "That's really all I have to do? Just clean four entire spaces for such short hours and a rather nice salary?"

"Yes, that's all, Miss Moore. You seem suspicious, as if there's something I'm not telling you."

I shake my head. "It just seems too good to be true. I don't even have any experience as a maid, except for cleaning my own house. And the pay is…"

Excessive.

"…substantial."

She nods her head. "You can thank the owner for that. He's a very generous man. I'm also too old to be climbing the stairs every day until the position is filled. Would you like the job?"

For crying out loud, I can't look a damn gift horse in the mouth. I need the money. I can't believe I'll be able to pay off all of my student loans cleaning someone's house.

A huge smile takes over my entire face. "Thank you so much. I would like it. I can start right away."

Emilia sighs. "That's wonderful, Miss Moore. And may I say a huge relief for me. Come with me and let me show you the essentials."

She rises from her chair and I do the same. We go back to the foyer and head up the stairs. A long narrow hallway runs the entirety of the second floor. She heads to a door and opens it, revealing a broom and a vacuum cleaner that from the looks of it is probably left over from the seventies.

"All you need to do up here is vacuum the hallway carpet once a week."

"That's all?"

"Yes. And all of these rooms are off limits," she informs me roughly.

"Of course. I understand."

"The owner does not like anyone intruding on his privacy," she adds for emphasis.

Her strict tone has me nodding, my eyes boring on hers. "I would never do that."

"Good," she replies curtly. "Let's go back downstairs."

The next stop is the guest bathroom, which only holds a toilet and a sink. But the cabinet over the sink intrigues me because it has a large empty space in its center, missing the mirror that should obviously be there.

"Who's the owner of this place? Dracula?"

Suddenly I realize I've said that out loud.

Shit.

Good-bye, easiest part-time job I ever would have had with a dream salary for just vacuuming a fucking hallway.

I turn around to look at Emilia, but her face doesn't read as angry. Her mouth is downturned, almost as if in sadness.

"I'm so sorry. I didn't mean it. I can go…"

I start to walk past her, but she grabs my forearm.

"It's all right. I know you didn't mean it. The owner just likes to keep to himself."

I bow my head briefly, embarrassed. "I understand. Forgive me."

Emilia nods silently to herself without looking directly at me. "Let me show you where the cleaning supplies are," she replies, almost more to herself than me.

Something in the tone of her voice makes me want to push further about the owner, whoever he or she is, but I decide I've said enough for one day.

The tour finally ends, and Emilia shows me to the door.

"You can start the day after tomorrow, if that suits your schedule. And wear whatever is comfortable. The owner doesn't require the staff to wear uniforms."

I glance at the woman, giving her clothes a once-over. She's dressed like she's stepped out of an Eileen Fisher catalog. "Very good. I'll see you then. And thank you again."

The woman holds out her hand to me. "Thank you, Lily."

I smile and shake her hand one last time.

Reaching my car, I shove my hand into my purse to rummage around for my keys. As I pull them out, something catches my attention in my peripheral vision. When I look up at the side of the house, a white silk curtain is fluttering behind a window on the second floor as if someone had been standing there and quickly backed away.

I stop for a minute to see if someone reappears, but the space remains empty. I push Ingrid's driver door once, twice, finally getting in to start her engine, which doesn't kick over.

"Come on, sweets. Please. It's been a long day and I just want to get the fuck home," I plead.

Finally, one more try and the engine roars to life. I exhale in relief.

I back out, glancing up one last time at the window. The curtain is still fluttering as I shift the car's gear into drive.

* * *

Walking into our house, I kick off my heels at the door. I drop my bag and head to the living room, collapsing onto the couch.

Heavy footsteps sound from the stairs. "Lily?"

"In here."

Reed appears in my sight, his eyes roaming over my clothes. "Why are you dressed like that?"

"I just had a job interview."

He sits down next to me, taking my feet into his lap. "And?"

"I got it."

"That's great, babe. What kind of job is it?"

"I'm a cleaning lady for some rich family."

He pauses then shakes his head; his mouth instantly draws into a frown. "Couldn't you find something better?"

I push my feet off his lap and sit up. "You know what the job market is like around here, Reed. I had to take what I could get. And it pays way more than minimum wage."

"I suppose that's all right," he mumbles. "Want to order pizza for dinner?"

Thanks for all the support, babe.

"Sure."

He rises to his feet. "I'll go call it in."

"Thanks."

I watch him walk into the kitchen, then stretch out on the sofa and stare up at the ceiling.

It's fine. He's probably just tired from work.

I get up and head upstairs to take a long, hot shower and wash the day off me.

Chapter Three

I cross the Rip Van Winkle Bridge from Columbia County to Greene County as I do once a week to visit my mom in Catskill. My heart leaps at the sight of the Hudson River below me, the rolling green hills of the Catskill Mountains in front of me, and a huge smile takes over my face. This is where my heart is.

Ahead of me, a black Jeep Wagoneer with a NURSES ROCK bumper sticker drives smoothly across the bridge. I honk my horn and wave to it. A hand appears from the driver's side window and waves back, then gives me a thumbs-up. I press my hand down on the horn once more and follow my mom back to our house.

We make the first left off the bridge at the light, past the Thomas Cole house. Thomas Cole was a member of the Hudson River School of painters, and my mom liked to take me there on Sundays to stroll through the gardens and take in the sweeping view. Reed's parents like to brag to their friends about my house being around the corner from it, *the* Thomas Cole, but of course, they've never actually visited it or my mother's house.

One more left turn, and I pull in behind my mom in our driveway. It's a simple two-story white clapboard house with a small front yard. A huge Christmas wreath hangs on the front door, and a single candle sits in each window. I always love how my mom goes all out at Christmas. She started doing this when I was five years old, to make me forget that my father had left us the year before.

My mom gets out of the Jeep, her blond hair pulled back in a ponytail. Under her long winter coat she's dressed in her nurse's scrubs and Mephisto clogs, and her hospital badge swings from her breast pocket: JOAN MOORE, RN-HUDSON COMMUNITY HOSPITAL-HEAD OF NURSING-ER. "Hi, sweetpea!"

I give her a tight hug. "What's going on? I thought you'd just be getting up."

"They needed me to come in last night because they were short-staffed. Huge ten-car pileup on the Thruway."

"Was it bad?"

"No fatalities, thank goodness. Come on, I'm starving. You can cook your mom breakfast."

I wrap my arm around her shoulders. "Deal."

Walking into the house, familiar smells permeate my nose—cinnamon because Mom bakes to relax, lemon from the cleanser she uses on the kitchen counters, and lily of the valley from the perfume she wears every day, to counter the antiseptic smell of the hospital, and the source of my first name.

I head straight to the kitchen to start cooking, popping bread in the toaster, turning on the kettle for Mom's mint tea, and then whisking eggs in a bowl for the scrambled eggs.

A sudden knock at the back door makes me smile. "Let her in, Mom."

I hear the sound of the screen door opening and excited voices fill the kitchen. "Add two more eggs for me, Lil."

A hint of patchouli wafts up to my nose. My best friend and next door neighbor since I was ten—Skylark "Sky" Rose—hugs me with one arm as I keep whisking.

I shake my head at her. "How have you gotten this far in life and your parents still haven't figured out that you gave up being vegan?"

"Because I come to your house to indulge in the forbidden fruits of meat, eggs, dairy, and sugar. Have you ever tried fair trade dark chocolate? Blech! Tastes like sandpaper."

Sky's parents, Bodhi and Haven, own the only health food store in town. The Bountiful Earth attracts the hippie and bohemian demographic from across the river in Hudson and even farther south, from Kingston and Woodstock, because they're known for being legit organic, earth to table, and all of the other buzzwords associated with being one with the planet.

It took my mom some time to get used to them when they first moved in, especially one day when she was mowing the lawn and Bodhi was outside sunbathing nude. She didn't mind him and Haven practicing tai-chi every morning with the dawn, but putting your junk on full display in front of your neighbor, who had a young daughter? Let's just say there's now a waist-high partition of bushes between our two houses that discreetly keep things hidden but still maintain the friendly neighbor vibe between us and the Roses.

I glance down at Sky's arms. "New tat?"

She runs her hand over her right forearm, the black-chipped polish on her fingernails contrasting the indigo blue of the fresh ink illustrating an ocean wave. "Yeah, it calms me down. Brings me back to my place of Zen."

"Mmm, I know the feeling," I observe, my mind flashing to *The Lovers*. "How's Kane?"

Her face softens with a warm look, the one she always gets whenever her boyfriend of two years is mentioned, who she met when he came to pick up his sister from the yoga studio where Sky works in Catskill. He rode up on his Harley, shoved his helmet under his arm, and dropped it the second he laid eyes on Sky's brilliant red silky hair and bright green eyes. "He's lovely. We're going out for a ride later. So, what's going on with you?"

Mom comes in, dressed in her sweats and wool socks. "My thoughts exactly. Talk to us while we set the table."

I pour the egg mixture into a heated pan, fluffing them as they cook. "In a nutshell, my ESL class was taken away from me because of budget cuts."

"Oh, honey, I'm so sorry. But I know you'll find something. You always land on your feet," Mom offers in encouragement.

"Funny you should mention that, Ma. I'm still going to be teaching in the spring, but only as an after-school tutor. So I went to the career services office on campus, and I took a part-time job as a cleaning woman."

"See!" Sky exclaims. "You're a rock star. Getting a job so quickly, especially with the lack of jobs in this area."

Sigh. That's the kind of reaction I wanted from Reed.

I grin back at her. "Thanks. And the best part is that it's going to give me a sweet paycheck in return. It'll help me pay off my student loans quicker."

"That's awesome, honey. And how is Reed handling it?" Mom asks.

"Well, he's not thrilled at the prospect of me not being the good girlfriend waiting for him when he gets home with his robe and slippers."

I hear my mom loudly plonk the plates down on the table. "You're shitting me!"

Yup, that's my mom. Joanie Moore. The strongest woman I know. Made of steel with a kind soul, but curses like a sailor. A single mother who doesn't put up with anything or anyone that messes with her kid. And I love her for it.

"No. I wish I were."

I hear the metal of cutlery clatter as Sky sets the utensils next to the plates. "Ha! Next thing you know, he'll want you barefoot and pregnant at twenty-four, ready to pop out the perfect 2.5 blond, blue-eyed kids."

"Couldn't have said it better myself, Skylark," my mom concurs. "Now what about your job? Palmer couldn't do anything?"

I continue fluffing the eggs. "It was a school board decision, Mom. He had no choice. He was actually really sorry about it."

She nods at me. "I get it. Okay, so tell me about this cleaning job."

I turn off the gas, lifting the pan, and spoon the eggs onto the plates. "It's…interesting."

"Why do you say that?" Sky asks.

"Well, it's in this old crumbling mansion on a hill not too far from Cottage Grove. The woman who takes care of the house is very nice. Emilia. Older with silver hair. And I haven't met the owner. But it's part-time, only twice a week, and it pays unbelievably well."

"Sounds creepy to me. But I guess if the money is that good, then you should do it," Sky says.

Mom sighs. "I suppose that's all right. But what I don't like is Reed's reaction. He has a huge stick up his ass. I don't know what you see in him."

Not again.

My shoulders drop at the sound of my mother's disapproval, something she's done before when it comes to Reed.

"Mom, please. Not now."

She reaches out to touch my shoulder. "He doesn't deserve you, honey. You know you can always come to me if you need any help financially. And this will always be your home, so if you ever feel like cutting the cord with him…"

"I'll hand you the scissors," Sky ends my mother's thought.

I shut my eyes in frustration. "Look, you two, I love that you're worried about me, but he loves me. And I'm fine now since I got the job. For the little work I'll be doing, the salary is very decent."

Am I going to have this argument for the rest of my life?

The whistle of the kettle jolts us, thankfully interrupting them. "Mom, please. Don't forget we're still spending Christmas Day with you, so I hope you won't bring all this up when he's here."

"Okay," she sighs. "I'll let it go for now because I'm starving. And then I can tell you all about the patient who had this thing sticking out of—"

Sky cringes in disgust, while I hold up my hand to my mother, palm facing front, my shoulders hunching in distaste. "Yuck! Mom, we're about to eat."

She laughs. "I know. I just wanted to bring you back, sweetpea. I promise I won't bring Reed up again. I only went on about him because I don't want to see you hurt."

"Same here," Sky agrees with a mouthful of egg.

I kiss Mom on the cheek, then bring my arm around Sky's shoulder to embrace her. "I know. Thanks, you guys. I love you both."

"Love you too, honey," Mom replies. "Now tell me who I have to call on the school board so I can read them the riot act for fucking with my kid."

I embrace her once more and smile to myself.

My mom, Joanie. The nurse warrior.

Chapter Four

Dipping the wet mop in the bucket, I pull it out and slap it down on the tiled kitchen floor on the first day at my new job. The job where I've only met Emilia, the combination caretaker/ estate manager/personal assistant; I don't even know what her official title is. This is my second task of the day. My first was to vacuum the rug in the upstairs hallway with the antiquated cleaner she'd shown me when I was here for the interview, and then I fully understood why the previous maid tripped bringing it down the stairs. It's one of those models with a round base on four wheels. I make a mental note to ask Emilia if the owners could possibly upgrade to an upright one at the very least.

Emilia steps out from her office off the kitchen. "I'll be leaving soon to run to the post office and pick up something for dinner. Will you be all right until I return?"

"Sure, but doesn't the owner have a chef on staff?"

She shrugs her shoulders. "What can I say? He prefers my cooking. And he doesn't like having more staff than necessary."

I nod my head in understanding. "I see. Do you need me to do anything else?"

She shakes her head. "No, that's all that needs to be done today. I don't want to overwork you on your first day, to the point where you quit."

"No chance of that," I reassure her, thinking of the ridiculous amount I'm being paid for so little work.

"Good. If you want, you can leave after you finish and I'll see you in a few days. You can just shut the front door behind you when you go."

"That would be great. Thank you. I'll see you then."

After a few more swipes across the floor, I assess my work and decide the floor is spotless. I wring out the mop and leave it in the laundry room to dry out, dumping the dirty water into the sink.

Stretching my aching back, I head from the kitchen to the living room. I sit down on one of the worn couches and lean back, sighing loudly to myself. I take only a minute to relax because otherwise I'll fall asleep on the spot.

When I sit up, I notice something through the French doors, a large object right in the center of the lawn. Emilia never said I couldn't go outside. I carefully turn the handle on one of the doors, listening to it creak as I pull it open and step through.

The backyard is wide and empty except for the object, which turns out to be a sculpture of a naked man in a seated position, crouched over and cradling his head in his hands. To my left there's a huge outbuilding in the shape of a barn, with a tall roof and wide doors that resemble ones that would usually be on a garage, and a long enclosed passageway that connects to the main house.

I slowly approach the sculpture. I take in the man's broad back, his long fingers as they cup his head, his muscled thighs tight under his chest. Something about it moves me; it seems so familiar, just like that sketch in the house, the pain and anguish of the subject akin to *The Lovers*.

It couldn't be…

I search for an artist's signature but I can't find one.

Maybe the house belongs to a wealthy art collector?

Suddenly, sounds of something being pounded and deep grunts divert my attention to the barnlike structure. I step the few yards to the building and quietly knock on the door. I give it a minute, but nobody appears. I slowly push the door open, and when I do, my jaw drops and my eyes widen at the sight in front of me.

It's not a barn at all. It's an artist's studio. Scaffolding and ladders are scattered everywhere. A huge hydraulic lift takes up an entire corner. Boxes marked SCULPTING CLAY line one entire wall. Another wall holds various tools, like brushes and knives. Long wooden tables are covered in newspaper, charcoal pencils, and sketchpads.

But what takes my breath away are the pencil drawings hanging on a string right by the door, preliminary sketches of *The Lovers*…

Oh my God.

This house.

The "S" hanging over the front gate.

Those sketches in the house.

The sculpture.

I think… the owner of this house might be Grayson Shaw.

And the man hunched over a mound of clay, pounding it into shape right in front of me, barefoot and clad only in a pair of ripped jeans, is him. It has to be. Grayson Shaw.

I can't look away from him. The rippling muscles of his back. His well-defined arms as they work the clay into submission. His skin, slick with sweat. His dark brown hair, which seems to slightly curl on top. I'm enraptured by the grunts that emanate from him with each movement.

The artist at work.

I'm mesmerized.

I can't believe…

"What the fuck do you think you're doing?"

I jump at the sound of his voice.

His dark brown eyes sear into mine, molten with fury. But then I gasp—one side of his face is beautiful, with chiseled cheekbone and lips, but the other is marked by three long scars starting from his forehead and extending all the way to his chin.

My entire body starts to shake and my mouth goes dry. "I…I…Are you Grayson Shaw?"

"Get the hell out of here!"

With my heart pounding against my chest, I rush out of the studio as fast as I can. I fly through the French doors into the living room, slamming into the sofa, grabbing it to keep myself standing as I pant for breath.

"Oh my goodness! What's happened?"

I look to my right, where Emilia is standing. I point toward the backyard. "Is he…was that…"

The older woman exhales, then purses her lips together as she nods in silent understanding. "You met him, didn't you?"

"If you're talking about the man in the studio, then yes." I finally catch my breath. "Emilia, do I work for Grayson Shaw?"

She exhales again. "Yes. Do you want to quit now that you've met him? Judging by your state, I'm assuming he did not treat you kindly."

My face turns red at her assumption. "He was…he was angry. I interrupted him in his studio. But I won't quit. Emilia, I need this job. Is he going to fire me for bothering him?"

Emilia inhales deeply, taking a few steps toward me, and pats my shoulder. "Leave it to me. I'll smooth things over. Why don't you go home? I think you've had enough for one day."

My shoulders drop in relief, my hands and legs still shaking.

Thank God. I can't get out of here fast enough.

***

GRAYSON

Run.

That's what they all do.

I can't blame them.

I'm a freak show.

I slide the gloss over the piece that arrived this morning. Thank God for the local artists' colony, which is always willing to pick up my pieces for baking; otherwise I'd never be able to do it myself.

That's not true. I have enough money. I could have an oven built here to handle the oversize ones. Something to think about.

Now I ensure every inch, every corner is covered, taking my time, making sure everything is perfect.

Perfect. Something I'll never be. A word I only associate with my art, certainly not myself. But she was perfect.

I can't believe Emilia hired her. What was she thinking? To bring someone so beautiful and innocent into this house of horrors?

I watched her from the window as she got into her car—or at least tried to—until she hip-checked the driver's door so she could actually open it. She obviously doesn't have the money to buy a new one, which must be the reason she took this job in the first place.

I step back to take in what I have completed. I exhale a breath of satisfaction.

As I clean the brush and secure the lid on the can of gloss, I stop as my mind wanders back to her. To Lily.

Someone like her could never understand true pain. She's probably never experienced it.

I want someone like her to see beyond my scars and know the real me.

But I would never expect any of that.

I know better.

But she works here now. It's just been Emilia and me for so long. Emilia's the one who deals with the staff. I'll have to get used to seeing Lily, and she'll have to adjust to my scars.

I glance at the table with my brushes, pencils, and sketches.

Damn it all to hell! Why must I resemble an act in a carnival sideshow?

I roar in a rage, clearing the table with one swipe of my arm.

I collapse to the floor, my heart pounding, trying to pump fresh oxygen into my lungs.

My head sinks into my hands.

When will I be normal?

The answer to my question flashes in my mind.

Never. A word I've come to know all too well.

Chapter Five

Y ou can't tell anyone about getting fired."

It's the night of the annual faculty holiday party at Ashby. Wearing a red knit dress that my mom lent me a few months ago, I turn away from our bathroom mirror to face Reed, my lip gloss in one hand, my jaw dropped. "Excuse me? First of all, I wasn't fired. I was reassigned. And second, why the hell not?"

"Because it would jeopardize my promotion if they think we might have to move for your career," he replies with a serious face.

"That makes no sense. If anyone should be embarrassed, it's the damn school board for denying a proper education for those students to whom English is a second language. Plus, these are academics, Reed. They'll understand about budget cutbacks."

His lips purse together and his eyebrows narrow in deep thought. "That's a good idea. That's how we'll spin it."

I shake my head. "We don't have to 'spin' anything, for fuck's sake. It's not like we're going to walk in there and announce to everyone, 'Hey, everyone, my girlfriend just lost her job.'"

Something's up with him.

I put my gloss down on the counter. He glares at me, his jaw tightly clenched. I reach out to touch his face. "Reed, babe, unclench, okay? What is going on? You know you can talk to me."

He exhales, shaking his head. "I'm just nervous. I met the new chair of the department today."

"So what's he like?"

"It's a 'she' actually. She's very intimidating. It's like when you're around her, you can't focus on anything else."

Huh. "I'm sure you were fine. She's going to be at the party, right?"

"Yeah." He pulls back on the cuff of his shirt, checking his watch. "Shit. Hurry up. We're going to be late."

I watch him rush from the bathroom as if his life depends on it.

Christ. Who's this woman who's got my boyfriend's boxers in a fucking twist?

"Lily!" he shouts from the bottom of the staircase.

I roll my eyes. "Relax! I'm coming!"

I grab my clutch and coat from the bed. When I reach Reed, I gasp at the sight of him holding out both of his hands to me, cradling a long red velour box.

"What's going on? Is this the reason you wanted me to hurry?"

"Yes…well, one of them anyway. Go on," he insists.

I take the box from him and gently open it. A necklace of white gold holding a single diamond in its center stares back at me.

I gasp. "Reed, I don't know what to say. Thank you."

He comes around me. "Let me put it on you."

I lift the back of my hair, leaning my head forward as he clasps the necklace around me. He leads me to the mirror by the front door, holding onto my shoulders.

"You look gorgeous."

My eyes tear up at his compliment. "What made you get this for me?"

He sighs. "I've been a douche, and I'm willing to admit it. So let's go have a good time, okay?"

I nod as he helps me into my coat.

"Thank you," I tell him again, genuinely touched.

"I have my moments."

Too few of them lately, but I'll take it.

Locking the door behind us, I watch him pull the protective tarp off his BMW, coming back around to help me into the car.

When we reach the campus, he takes my hand, keeping it clasped with his as we make our way to the admin building where the party is being held.

A young girl takes our coats at the door and then we're greeted by the president of the college and chairs of the various departments, with Reed taking ages talking to every one of them.

When he's drawn into a chat about the budget for the computer science department, I excuse myself, nearly bumping into someone carrying a tray of canapés.

"Oh, I'm so sorry…Señora Rojas?"

Dressed in a waiter's uniform of a button-down white shirt, black tie, and a black skirt, a short woman with soft brown eyes smiles at the sight of me.

"*Sí.* Hello, Miss Lily. It is so nice to see you. How are you?"

"I'm fine, thank you. It's lovely to see you. I have to tell you how pleased I am that Esperanza is doing so well in class."

She beams like the proud mother she is. "*Gracias*. I'm so happy to hear—"

"Lily."

Reed's stern voice interrupts us.

I turn to him. "Reed, this is Mrs. Rojas. Her daughter is in my class, and she's one of my top students. She won the class spelling bee last week."

He grabs me by my wrist, allowing a small grin of acknowledgement. "That's wonderful. You must be very proud. Lily, I need you. Pardon us."

I look back at Mrs. Rojas, who looks at me like any mother would—her mouth downturned in sadness, her eyes narrowed in concern.

"It was lovely to see you, Señora Rojas," I manage to get out before Reed pulls me away. I disentangle myself from his grip and head for an empty corner of the room.

"You just embarrassed me in front of one of my class parents," I tell him through gritted teeth.

"And you were supposed to stay by my side and make a good impression. I wanted to introduce you to some important trustees."

"Reed, I'm not your damn puppet ready to put on a show whenever you command me. I'm your girlfriend. And Mrs. Rojas is just as important to me."

"Then act like it—my girlfriend, that is," he counters. "If I get this promotion, it means you can stop working altogether, especially working with kids who can barely speak English."

"But that's exactly the reason why—"

Before I can finish my point, he grabs me by the hand, hauling me back into the party, ready to play the good girlfriend.

I shut my eyes for a second.

What happened to the chivalrous gentleman? The one who less than an hour ago gifted me with a diamond necklace, assisted me with my coat, helped me in and out of the car, held my hand all the way here?

He steers us toward two couples, both sets emitting a haughty sense of entitlement, the kind I feel whenever I'm around Reed's parents.

"Ah, Reed, you found her," one of the silver-haired women says.

Reed shifts his hand from mine to encircle my waist, tugging me closer to him. When I glance at him, his face is plastered with the smile I've seen a thousand times—the one he wears when he's trying to impress someone.

"Yes, ma'am. May I introduce my girlfriend, Lily Moore? Lily, these are…"

I instantly forget their names, knowing he's only doing this for his own career. My anger from his treatment of Mrs. Rojas is still percolating.

I shake everyone's hands as one of the patrician-looking men addresses me. "So, what do you do?"

It always comes down to that in this type of circle. Who you know, what you do, the balance of your bank account.

"I was a schoolteacher, but—"

"But what?"

A flash of pain grabs my right side as Reed pinches the flesh on my hip.

Reed laughs uncomfortably. "What are you talking about, honey? She still is. The school is just going through a transition right now."

Eyebrows raise in comprehension, with a round of "I see" emitted from the group.

Puppet on a string. Just play along and you'll be home soon enough.

"Will you excuse me?"

Reed glares at me.

"I'll be right back. I just need to freshen up," I reassure him.

He nods reluctantly as I extricate myself from the group, walking as briskly as I can to the restroom.

I grab the counter, taking deep breaths to calm myself.

"Do you need anything, dear?"

I turn to my left, coming face to face with a grey-haired woman in a matron's uniform.

"I'm actually feeling a bit light-headed," I admit to her.

She takes me gently by the elbow and sits me down in a plastic chair near the hand dryer. I lean my head back against the cool of the tiled wall as she hands me a cup of water.

"Here. Take as long as you want."

I slowly nod. "Thank you."

I shut my eyes, allowing the cool liquid to relax my heated throat. Once I finish, I throw the empty cup into a trash bin, and slowly rise to my feet.

The matron glances over at me from the counter where she's wiping up around the sinks. "Better?"

"Yes, much. Thank you again."

When I return to the party, I search the room for Reed. My

eyes finally land on him, and my teeth instantly grit at the sight of him having a conversation with a tall, lithe woman dressed in an emerald green silk dress and silver stilettos, her dark brown hair falling like a silk curtain over her shoulders. One of her hands is on Reed's shoulder, holding it tightly as she whispers into his ear.

What the…

I hold my head up high, slapping a smile on my face as I approach. The woman pulls back, a smug grin across her face as I reach for his hand. "Reed, honey, I thought I lost you there for a minute. Will you introduce us?"

He clears his throat. "Umm…yeah…I mean yes. Lily, this is Tabitha Cross, the new chair of the computer science department. Dr. Cross, this is Lily Moore, my girlfriend."

She holds out her hand to me. "A pleasure."

Shit. Reed was right. No wonder he couldn't focus on anything else when he was in the room with her. Standing so confidently and self-assured, her spine ramrod straight and shoulders thrown back, she commands attention.

A shiver passes over me when I take her hand, her cold skin meeting my warm palm. "Likewise," I reply.

The woman and I stare at each other, clearly assessing each other. Her brown almond-shaped eyes roam over me, taking in my appearance.

The hairs on my neck rise against my skin. The intensity of her glare unnerves me, and I wish I knew why. But I can't help but smile when her eyes land on my neck.

"What a pretty…necklace," she offers.

I touch it lightly with my fingertips. "Reed gave it to me just before we left for the party."

"How…lovely," she replies.

My eyebrows rise in confusion.

What is this woman's problem?

My stomach begins to churn from unease. I place my hand on Reed's forearm. "Honey, I'd like to go home now."

He looks over at Dr. Cross before answering. "Umm, sure. Will you excuse us?"

"Of course. It was nice to meet you. I'll see you tomorrow, Reed," she tells him, her eyes narrowing on him before turning on her heel in the direction of the bar.

I tug on his jacket sleeve. "Let's go get our coats."

"Yeah," he replies absently, his eyes focused on Dr. Cross's back.

I take him by the hand, pressing it to get his attention. Finally he switches back to me, following me to the coat check.

Reed helps me with my coat as we bundle up to face the cold. His gloved hand takes mine when we step outside.

I swallow before asking, "So that's your new chair?"

"Yeah. Why?"

"I was just wondering. Is she married?"

He guides me around a patch of ice on the pavement. "No. I think she's divorced, but I'm not sure. What's with the twenty questions?"

"It's not twenty. She just seemed very attentive toward you, that's all."

"Why wouldn't she be? She's the head of my department."

"I just thought…"

"What?"

I clear my throat.

Just say it.

"It looked like she was flirting with you."

Suddenly Reed releases my hand. I walk ahead of him but lose my balance on a patch of ice and slip onto the frozen ground.

Pain shoots from my palms up my arms to my shoulders and from my knees up my thighs to my hips.

Reed rushes to me. "Shit! Lily, are you okay?"

I wince from the pain. "Yeah. Just help me up."

He takes me gently by my elbows as I slowly rise to my feet, guiding me away from the ice.

Then he looks at my neck.

I glance at him suspiciously. "What?"

"Your necklace. It's still there."

I gasp in disgust. "It's not my necklace that got hurt, Reed. It's my hands and knees, but thank you for your concern."

He shakes his head at me. "Let's just go."

We don't speak for the entirety of the drive home, and I realize he never replied to my suspicions about Dr. Cross flirting with him.

When we walk through our front door, he suddenly grabs me by the hips.

"Come on, baby…"

His hot breath wafts over my neck from behind. Combined with the spicy scent of his cologne, a wave of nausea overtakes me. His hands roam over my chest, pushing his palms hard into my breasts, squeezing my nipples to the point of pain.

I push his hands off my chest. "No, Reed. Not tonight. Not like this. I don't feel well."

"I want it."

I grab him by the wrists and hold them at my sides. "Well, that makes one of us."

He pulls away from me and I turn around to face him. His eyes are angry. "Do you realize you turn me down more than we actually do it?"

"I don't feel well. Maybe tomorrow, okay?"

I walk away without waiting for his reply.

I slowly head up the stairs to the bedroom, carefully removing my clothes as my arms and legs protest in pain. I slip into my bathrobe and slippers, making my way back down to the living room, where Reed has collapsed on the couch, snoring loudly. I pad to the kitchen, filling the kettle and prepping my mug with a chamomile teabag.

"What the fuck do you think you're doing?"

Grayson Shaw suddenly enters my mind.

What the...

Why am I thinking about him? He wasn't at all what I was expecting. He's definitely not the most pleasant person. Then again, he wasn't expecting someone to interrupt him when he was working.

However, given the physical appearance of his face, I can certainly understand why he lashed out at me. He's not used to intruders.

But the rest of him...his overwhelming presence, the way his hulking body took up so much space in his studio, how he loomed over me, his deep, husky voice.

My entire body warms at the thought of it all.

The sound of the kettle whistling snaps me out of my recollection. I turn off the stove and prepare my tea, sitting back down at the table with my hands wrapped around the hot, steaming mug, watching as a light flurry of snow falls outside.

I shut my eyes at the thought of his scars, now realizing why he's never been seen in public. I don't know what caused them, and as much as I want to know I don't think he'll want any pity or sympathy from me.

But I do know I'll have to give him something when I go back to work tomorrow—an apology for intruding on his privacy and running away like a frightened animal.

I take a deep breath and steel myself mentally for that moment.

He doesn't deserve you, honey.

My mother's words run through my mind on a loop.

I take another sip of my tea as the snow continues to fall.

Chapter Six

I knock quietly on Emilia's office door the next day. I'm dressed for work in my Ashby College sweats and a cream turtleneck. I realized the last time I was here that central heating doesn't come with the house.

The older woman opens the door, a cell phone plastered to her ear. She holds up a single finger to me, indicating she'll be with me in a minute. "No, that's not good enough. We need the truck to be here by noon at the latest so it can meet the plane at Logan in time for the flight to Heathrow. Yes, I can wait."

She sighs in exasperation at me and shakes her head, but manages to give me a quick grin. "Grayson's got a show in London. He's sending two large pieces, and this putz is telling me the sculptures won't make the flight tonight from Boston to London."

I tilt my head in confusion. "He's not...going, is he?"

She gives me a sympathetic look. "No, dear. They're just shipping two of his sculptures, that's all."

I silently nod my head.

Emilia speaks into the phone again. "Yes? Excellent. We'll see you then."

She ends her call and drops the phone to her desk. "Thank God that's done."

She sits down in her desk chair, gesturing for me to take the other seat in her office.

I sit as she carefully folds her hands on her desk. She glances over at a picture on her desk, of a young couple dressed elegantly and smiling widely, the woman holding a toddler in her arms. When she notices my eyes on it, a wistful look crosses her face.

"I've worked for the Shaw family since Grayson was born. He's like a son to me. What happened to him as a boy is just…" She trails off, shaking her head

Don't ask.

Do. Not. Ask.

She stares at the picture. "He was five years old when it happened. He and his parents were returning from a weekend trip. The weather was similar to what it is now. They hit a patch of black ice and their car went over the hill. His parents were killed instantly. He was in the back seat, still wearing his seat belt when he was pulled out."

My gaze shifts to the picture, tears forming in the corners of my eyes.

Emilia reaches out to tap me gently on my right hand to get my attention. "Lily, if you're worried about your job, don't be. I have no cause to fire you. And even if I wanted to, Grayson would object."

Suddenly, a sense of warmth envelops my entire body, as

if someone had just covered me with a cashmere blanket. "Why?"

"Because he told me what happened in his studio from his perspective and when I asked what he wanted me to do about it, he said 'Nothing.'"

The warmth dissipates as quickly as it overtook me. Her reply unnerves me, leaving me cold and with a sense of disappointment that I wish I could understand.

"All I can say is just stay out of his way and don't go into his studio uninvited," she continues.

I nod in relief and understanding. "Of course. Thank you."

She claps her hands together. "Right. Today I need you to polish the silver. I apologize because I know that sounds very *Downton Abbey* of me, but even though Grayson could care less about the house, I do. And I think it's important to take care of precious things, don't you?"

I wonder if she's talking about Grayson. "Yes, it is. Which silver?"

"Oh, just the items on the mantel in the living room and whatever is on the sideboard in the dining room."

"I'll get to it then."

"I'll be upstairs if you need anything," she informs me.

I follow her out of the office. She heads upstairs while I go to the supply closet. I easily find the silver polish, but I can't see the rags anywhere.

My cell phone jolts me when it rings in the pocket of my sweats.

I hurriedly swipe it open. "Reed, I can't talk now. I'm working."

"Did you do something to the printer? I'm running late and I need to print out a doc for class."

"No, I didn't do anything to the printer. I can't even remember the last time I used it."

"Are you sure?" he insists.

"I'm fucking positive. I'm not an idiot. Just print it out when you get to campus. Look, I have to go," I snap back at him.

"I never said you were an idiot."

I grit my teeth together. "I don't need this shit right now, least of all from my own boyfriend. You know I need this job. We'll talk when I get home."

I end the call, shoving the phone back into my pocket, sighing in frustration.

A deep voice from behind me asks, "Are you in need of something?"

I jump up and gasp, clasping my right hand over my heart, beating rapidly from the shock. I slowly turn around, now face to face with Grayson. Dressed in a black crewneck sweater stretched across his chest by his powerful muscles, and worn jeans that cover his long legs, his dark brown eyes bore into mine. His chest rises up and down from what I can only imagine is impatience as he waits for my answer.

"I was looking for the rags to polish the silver," I reply breathlessly. "I'm sorry if you overheard—"

"Were you raised by wolves?"

I shake my head at the peculiarity of the question. "Excuse me?"

"You entered my studio without permission, which is why I'm asking if you were raised in a forest by animals."

Is this guy for real?

I take a deep breath to calm myself. "No, Mr. Shaw. I was raised by a single mother who worked day and night to make sure I had a decent life and received a college education. But I thought a person like you would have better manners."

His shoulders slump as his gaze shifts to the floor. He doesn't say a word as I continue.

"I'm very sorry for intruding on your privacy. I was exploring the grounds and I realize now that was a mistake. I should've asked Emilia's permission first. But I just have to tell you that I love your sculpture on campus. I went to Ashby for my undergrad and whenever I needed some peace, I always sat by *The Lovers* and it was like my sanctuary. It still is, and I love—"

"Enough!"

I jump in place from his sudden outburst, gasping yet again in surprise. I didn't even realize I was rambling.

"You're just saying that to be nice so you don't lose your job and because of what I look like. The way you screamed at me when you first saw me in the studio and your reaction, running away like a scared little girl, was rude and offensive."

This man is unbelievable.

I take a step toward him to disprove his theory. This close, he towers over me and I have to pivot my head up to look into his eyes. My knees begin shaking, but then I detect the scent of body wash from him, fresh and clean, which somehow calms my nerves. I clear my throat.

"Mr. Shaw, with all due respect, I'm not a scared little girl. And I didn't scream. I gasped. I wasn't expecting to find anyone inside, but more to the point, to see an injury like yours. I had no idea what you looked like, so how did you expect me to react? Emilia didn't warn me about you. That's why I screamed, not because I found you ugly or hideous."

I watch as his face contorts in confusion, his eyebrows narrowed, his lips clenched as if to keep himself in check.

"Why did you take this job?"

I inhale deeply. "I lost my job. I teach ESL at Cottage Grove School and the board decided that they didn't need to have separate ESL classes. I won't be teaching full-time next semester, but I'll still be tutoring my students in the afternoon. They're amazing kids. I love seeing them learn and the joy on their faces just from being in school."

I stop explaining and wait for him to say something, but he just continues to stare at me, making my legs shake nervously.

Finally, he speaks gruffly, gesturing to the cabinet next to the kitchen sink. "I see. The rags are in there."

I watch as he storms off toward the side door in the kitchen, which I now realize leads to the passageway that connects his studio to the main house.

A wave of sadness envelops my entire body. I mentally review everything I just said to him. I don't think I sounded insincere. As intimidating as he was physically the first time I saw him, all I've seen now is a man whose spirit is broken and only needs someone to pull the thorn from his paw.

Or he's just a self-absorbed artist who doesn't give a shit about other people's feelings.

I wonder about that the entire time I polish his family's silver until I can see my face reflected back at me in the precious metal.

* * *

GRAYSON

My hand slams into the clay, forcing it to submit to me.

Pound.

She was just being nice.

Pound.

I don't care how much she denied it.

That's all I can think about, the only thoughts that occupy my mind.

Sweat rolls down my back. My hair is plastered against my forehead. I don't even know what time it is. The sun went down long ago. I just needed to create something new, to vent this pent-up rage inside me. I blast Vivaldi's "Winter" with its furious violins on my stereo system, and the music perfectly matches my mood.

And then her face enters my mind.

I see the way her light blue eyes turned brighter as she took a step toward me, unafraid to confront me. I see her creamy skin turn from its usual pinkish hue to bright red as she spoke to me, so determined, with no fear.

She didn't flinch once. She didn't cringe.

The way she spoke about her mother—so proud, so loving. I couldn't look at her when she was talking about her because I was so ashamed.

My arms drop from the sculpture, my muscles aching for rest.

I sink to the floor, my body completely spent but my head still full of her.

And that phone call…it was her boyfriend. Reed, I think. How she talked to him. I haven't even met him, and already I know he doesn't treat her in the manner she deserves.

A loud knock sounds at the door.

I rise from the floor. When I open the door, Emilia stands on the other side holding a dinner tray in her hands.

"Your dinner, Grayson." Her eyes take in my appearance. "Is everything all right?"

"Yes," I mumble in reply.

She gives me a slight smile and hands me the tray. "Have a good evening. I'll see you in the morning."

Holding my dinner in my hands, I call out to her retreating back. "Emilia."

She turns around to face me. After what Lily revealed to me, I need to make sure of something.

"No matter what happens, Miss Moore keeps her job."

She nods. "Of course, Grayson. Understood."

I shut the door, taking the tray of steaming food over to one of my worktables. I sit down on a tall stool, glancing down at my dinner.

I take a deep breath.

I shouldn't have snapped at Lily the way I did. She was just defending herself, and why she walked into my studio. From what she told me, she obviously had a rough childhood. And even though I've lost my parents, at least I don't have to worry about losing my home or not having enough to eat because my parents ensured I was taken care of.

I truly am a beast.

Chapter Seven

Slamming Ingrid's trunk shut in my driveway, I haul two over-flowing bags of groceries into my arms. I reach the door but can't manage to get the key in the lock from being so overloaded. I use my elbow to ring the bell over and over until Reed appears in the doorway.

"Why didn't you just use your key?"

My jaw drops at his cluelessness. "You're joking, right?"

At least he's enough of a gentleman to take the bags from me. "What took you so long?"

I follow him into the kitchen. "For crying out loud, Reed, it's not my fault the supermarket was having a sale on Christmas turkeys. It was beyond crowded. Do me a favor, please. Nuke the rotisserie chicken and set the table. I'll make the baked potatoes and salad when I come down. I have to go change."

I hear him mumble under his breath about doing it during the next commercial break as I walk out, leaving my wet snow boots at the door before I head upstairs.

When I return to the kitchen a few minutes later, Reed is pouring white wine into glasses. Plates, cutlery, and napkins are already laid out on placemats on the table.

I give him a peck on the cheek. "Thank you. I had a tough day."

He shrugs his shoulders in reply.

I head for the kitchen, pulling the lettuce out to rinse it.

Why he didn't want to know about my day?

I chop two tomatoes for the salad.

Why don't I want to know how his day went?

I pop the potatoes in the microwave.

Am I afraid of his answer if I do ask?

The ping of the microwave brings me back to the present. I take out the potatoes and bring them to the table, where Reed is already sitting, waiting for me before he serves himself.

I return to the kitchen for the dressing, the salad, the sour cream and the butter, glancing at Reed, who doesn't move an inch to help me carry any of the food.

Reed and I go through the motions as I take a long sip of wine and carve a thigh from the chicken. Then, taking some salad and a potato, I dig into my dinner.

I stare across at my boyfriend, who's perfectly dressed in a long-sleeved polo shirt, not a blond hair out of place. He cuts his food so meticulously that he could be a surgeon performing an operation, every move precise. The silence in the room is deafening.

What is happening to us?

I can't look at him anymore because suddenly, I think of Grayson and how perfectly imperfect he is. It's such a cruel joke how one side of his face is deformed by jagged scars, the other intact, untouched by tragedy. Now I know why he has no mirrors in his house.

"Lily!"

Reed's impatient voice snaps me back to the dinner table. "What?"

"I've been trying to get your attention for ages. What's going on with you?"

I sigh to myself. "Did you not hear me tell you I had a tough day?"

He closes his eyes. "Sorry. I wasn't thinking. What happened?"

I put down my fork and knife. "It's the man I work for. He has a horrible injury."

"What kind of injury?"

"I can't say. It's just…very sad."

He chews his food slowly, then reaches for his wine. "Christ, Lily, it's just a job. And doesn't he live in a mansion or something like that? He's probably fine. If he's living in a mansion, I'm sure he's got some good insurance."

"Excuse me?"

"I don't get why you're acting so weird. It's not like you're married to him. All you do is clean his house. That's what you should care about more, not what he looks like. Sounds like he's well off, so I wouldn't feel so badly for him if I were you."

I bite down on my inner lower lip to both keep me from yelling at him for his lack of compassion.

"I can't believe you," I whisper to myself.

I stare down at my food, suddenly feeling nauseous. I push the plate away, grab my wine glass, and push back from the table. "I need to be alone."

"Lily, what the hell?"

I stare back at him, my eyes and voice unwavering. "Please take care of the dishes and the leftovers."

I hear him grunt with displeasure behind me as I walk out, not looking back once.

Once upstairs, I sit in the bay window. I don't know how much time passes before I hear footsteps coming up the stairs. When I glance over, Reed is standing in the doorway holding a glass of wine.

"I'm sorry," he whispers, looking forlorn. "Can I give you a foot rub, then maybe take you out for a nightcap? I think we both need one."

Exhaling a deep breath, I agree. "Sure."

He places his wine glass on the dresser and settles himself onto the seat, taking my feet into his hands, rubbing them from heel to toes, making sure each is properly massaged. I fall back into the soft cushions behind me, taking a long sip of wine. I close my eyes to absorb the sensations running from my feet, relaxing my nerve endings as I take deep, cleansing breaths.

I don't even notice when Reed releases my feet from his grip, placing them in his lap.

My eyes snap open, nodding at him. "Thank you. That felt good."

My cheeks begin to hurt when I return the grin on his face, from keeping it on mine for too long.

Sure, I'm relaxed now, and that was nice, but why do I still feel empty inside?

That question sticks in my head for the rest of the night, despite the fact that Reed's behavior reminds me of how he was when we first started dating. He opens doors for me, pushes my chair in at the local pub where we both order Irish coffees, gets up from his chair when I stand up to go to the restroom.

When I return to the table, he reaches out to take my hand. "I know I've been acting like a shit, Lily, and I'm so sorry. I've been so worried about my job and my observation that I forget about everything and everyone else."

The sincerity in his voice touches me to my core. "I forgive you. And I understand."

"Oh, my parents want to have us over for brunch on Sunday."

My good mood slowly dissipates. "Okay. That would be nice."

He kisses the knuckles on my hand. "Thank you, honey. I promise from now on I'll be the perfect boyfriend."

He releases my hand to signal for our waitress.

Perfect.

Hearing him use that word jolts me as I stare back at him, wondering what the term *perfect* means to him.

And before I can stop myself, my mind fills with the image of Grayson's face, so perfectly imperfect.

* * *

The next day at Grayson's I call out to Emilia but nobody responds. I check the kitchen counter, finding a list of chores from her. When I go to the supply closet to hang up my coat, something catches my attention from the corner of my eye.

Sitting on top of the cleaning supplies is a postcard. When I pick it up, I smile to myself. It's one of those postcards you find in a museum. *The Lovers* stare back at me.

I turn it over. A message is written in elegant penmanship:

Lily,

Please come see me in my studio today after you've finished work.

Thank you,
GS

My eyebrows narrow in worry.

Fuck. What did I do now?

I tuck the postcard into my purse and grab the mop bucket with shaking hands, eager to finish my chores so I can face Grayson and get it over with.

* * *

GRAYSON

A quiet knock sounds on the door.

When I answer it, Lily stands in the passageway. "Hello. You asked to see me."

Her hands are clutched together, and she's nervously tangling her fingers. "Don't worry. Nothing's wrong," I reassure her. "Please come in."

I step back and watch her enter. She's dressed in a black ribbed turtleneck and sweatpants with the word "Ashby" embossed across her backside, making me smile for a brief moment.

Very amusing. She graduated from Ashby. I like that.

I gesture to my desk chair. "Please sit down."

She nods silently and settles herself as I pull up a stool from one of my worktables.

"So, you like *The Lovers*."

A wide grin envelops her face. She leans back in the chair and clears her throat. "Um…yes. Yes, I do."

"You called it your 'sanctuary.' What do you like most about it?"

She tilts her head before replying. "Whenever I'm having a bad day, that's where I go to clear my head. I forget everything that's going on and focus on the sculpture…her long hair, the hem of her dress as if it's actually waving, the pain the man must be in to need that kind of comfort."

I nod as she bites her lower lip. "What is it?"

She shakes her head. "No, forget it."

"It's all right, Lily. Ask me."

Suddenly, her eyes fix on mine. "What was…I mean…what made you create that? You don't have to answer if it's too personal."

I breathe in deeply, giving her a brief smile. "I don't mind, Lily. All art is personal. *The Lovers* was one of my first sculptures. It was incredibly cathartic for me, working on it, that is. I never truly addressed my parents' death, and it just helped me express a lot of emotions that I hadn't faced until then."

"Emilia told me about your parents," she whispers. "I'm so sorry."

"Thank you for that. And thank you for your thoughtfulness about asking me. But tell me, do you do anything when you're there? I mean, do you just sit and stare at it?"

She laughs quietly. "Sometimes, but I like to take pictures of it. Close-ups, really."

I lean back on the stool with my mouth agape, surprised by her confession. "I wasn't expecting that. Would you let me see them?"

She sits up as her jaw drops, completely beguiling me. "Really?"

"Of course. I'd love to see my work through someone else's view."

"They're on my Nikon at home. I'll bring it with me next time."

"I'd enjoy that."

Silence permeates the room as we sit grinning at each other. But then, a cold realization hits me…I'm smiling. When have I ever smiled so much?

The newness of the emotion sends me reeling.

I jump to my feet. "Yes…well…" I stammer, "You're probably tired and would like to go home."

She laughs again, rising from the chair. "I do, but I really enjoyed talking to you. Thank you for the postcard and for the invitation."

"You're welcome. Here, let me get the door for you."

When she reaches me, she turns to me with another grin. "Thank you, Mr. Shaw."

"It was my pleasure. And please call me Grayson."

She nods. "Good night, Grayson."

I swallow. "Good night, Lily."

I close the door behind her, slamming my back to it.

I am such a fool. Babbling like that in front of her. What she must think of me.

I take a few steps to the back table and stare at my work in progress. Something about it doesn't feel right.

I mash the clay together, eliminating all traces of what was there.

And then I start over.

Chapter Eight

"Did you read that article in the latest issue of *Fortune* about the Top Ten father-son businesses in America?"

"My DAR chapter is planning the most glorious benefit."

"I think it's time I upgraded to the newest BMW series."

I sit at the dining table of Charles and Adeline Shepard silently eating the lobster bisque that Mrs. Shepard had her personal chef prepare as Mr. Shepard, Mrs. Shepard, and Reed engage in brunch conversation on the most boring topics.

Ever since Reed and I started dating, I've learned that Mrs. Shepard never steps foot in the kitchen. Every appetizer, entrée, side dish, and dessert is either cooked by her chef or ordered from the finest gourmet grocery store in Saratoga Springs. Even Whole Foods is beneath Adeline's standards, and forget about Trader Joe's.

The fine crystals in the limestone of their stately home sparkled in the sun when we pulled up this afternoon, no doubt from the power washing that I'm sure Mrs. Shepard ordered before today. Everything about the house is perfect, the kind of home where one would be afraid to touch something for fear of breaking it.

To me, this house is a mausoleum. There is nothing alive about it, no spirit. I suffocate from the atmosphere alone. Reed's parents sit at either end of the table, while Reed and I are seated across from each other in the center. The conversation numbs my mind. I have nothing to contribute to it. Politics and religion are never discussed because both are considered taboo and distasteful as conversation topics.

What is Grayson doing for Christmas? He probably never celebrates it. He was so sweet with me in his studio, the way he got nervous at the end before I left…

"Lily."

The sound of my name crossing Mrs. Shepard's lips snaps me out of my musings.

"I'm so sorry. Yes, ma'am?"

"I asked how your teaching job was going."

I glance across the table at Reed. His jaw is clenched, his green eyes searing into me, wordlessly warning me not to do it.

I don't care. I'm telling the truth.

"I lost my job, Mrs. Shepard. Budget cuts. I'm going to be an afterschool tutor for the spring semester, so at least I'll be teaching in some form. For now, I'm a part-time cleaning woman for a private client."

There's no way I'm giving away Grayson's identity because I know it would only impress them, and they'd want to know everything about him. I refuse to betray his privacy.

The mood in the room instantly changes. The chill becomes

palpable. Looks are exchanged between the Shepards, then they share a disdainful glare at their son. This seems mixed with disappointment that I read as if they are saying, *Oh, how could you, Reed? We simply can't have a cleaning woman in our family.*

Mr. Shepard clears his throat. "Well, it's temporary, I'm sure."

I look at Reed again. He gives his parents a reassuring smile. "Of course it's temporary. She's a great teacher. Aren't you, Lily?"

I grit my teeth, taking a deep breath, flashing the Shepards a smile so fake it hurts my facial muscles. "Thank you, Reed. Yes, I am."

* * *

"What were you thinking? Why did you tell them you were a maid? Do you know how embarrassing that was for me?"

Reed's booming voice echoes inside his car, vibrating off the glass. I simply sit with my hands folded in my lap, looking out the window.

"Will you answer me, for chrissakes?"

I turn my head to face him. "Your mother asked a question, and I answered it. I wasn't going to lie or sugarcoat anything. And I said I was a cleaning woman, not a maid."

He slaps the steering wheel with his leather-gloved hand. "Same difference. You could've just said you were in between jobs."

"I'm not a liar, Reed. I wasn't raised that way. My family isn't like yours, where everything is shoved under the rug."

"At least I was raised with manners. Your mother's language is offensive."

It's one thing to mess with me, but when it comes to my mother, the gloves come off.

"Don't you ever talk about my mother that way!"

With a screech, he pulls the car over, puts it in park, and grabs my wrist. "And don't you ever talk to me that way!"

Despite the soft leather of his glove, his fingers grip me so tightly that I shout in pain. Trying to pull out of his strong hold only increases the hurt.

"Damn it! Let go of me, Reed! You're hurting me!"

At the sound of my strangled voice, he instantly lets go. "I'm-I'm so sorry," he stutters. "I really am. My parents just bring out the worst in me sometimes."

I slowly rub my wrist to ease the pain. "I wish I knew why you act like this, Reed. One minute you're sweet and loving, and the next you're cruel and hurtful. Why are you like this with me now?"

He sighs audibly, grabbing the steering wheel harder. "I wish I knew too, honey. Maybe it's just the stress from work. I swear to you I'll do better. And I'm so sorry for hurting you like that." One of his hands reaches over to caress my left cheek. "You know I'm sorry, right?"

Looking straight ahead, I nod silently, his hand still holding my cheek. "Yes, I know that."

Despite having just eaten brunch, my stomach drops as if I hadn't consumed a morsel of food. Chills run up and down my arms. I wrap myself tighter in my coat.

Do I truly know that? Or am I just lying to myself?

* * *

GRAYSON

Going over my schedule in my diary as I sip my morning coffee, I take particular notice of the date.

Christmas. It's almost here. My least favorite holiday.

I try not to watch television during Christmas. Everyone is too cheerful, the movies are saccharine, and every film and TV show ends happily with the entire cast singing a carol.

I can't stand it. Despite Emilia's protests, I order her every year not to put up any Christmas decorations or a fucking tree. What would be the point? I'd only have one person to exchange gifts with, anyway.

Closing my diary, I pick up the breakfast tray Emilia brought over two hours ago to return it to the kitchen.

Once in the kitchen, I place it on the counter. I'm about to head back to the studio when I hear humming, then singing. "Hark! The Herald Angels Sing!"

Wonderful. A Christmas carol.

I follow the sound to the foyer, where I find Lily facing the windows that frame the front door, spraying them with cleaner, then wiping them, every move accompanied by singing or humming.

I sigh.

Too cheerful.

"You don't have to do that," I say to her back.

She jumps at the sound of my voice, instantly dropping the paper towel and bottle of window cleaner to the floor. "Oh my God!"

When she turns around, her face is slightly pink from activity, her hand raised to her chest. "I didn't hear you come in. I'm sorry if I was disturbing you."

She gives me a brief glance, then just as quickly looks away.

"You weren't disturbing me. I just don't think it's necessary for you to wash the windows. Did Emilia tell you to do that?"

"Yes."

"Well, you needn't bother. I think the windows are clean enough. Did you bring your camera?"

Her face lights up. "I did. But I still have to vacuum the upstairs hallway."

I shake my head. "The hallway isn't going anywhere. Get your camera and I'll meet you in the living room."

She nods with a smile. "Okay."

While she's retrieving her camera, I settle myself onto one of the sofas in the living room. She stops when she sees me, biting her bottom lip.

I need to ease her nerves. "Come show me what you have."

She leaves about a foot between us when she sits down next to me, silently handing over her camera, which I handle carefully. "Could you show me…"

Lily shakes her head. "Oh, right. Of course."

She moves closer, and the fresh scent of flowers wafts over me. I breath it in deeply, intoxicated. I glance at her as she presses a set of buttons on the camera. She probably wears the perfume to counter the antiseptic smells of cleaning products that she uses when she's here.

An image pops up on the screen: the face of the woman in *The Lovers*. The way Lily's captured her stuns me into silence.

A sprinkling of white snow presents a deep contrast against the dark stone of the sculpture.

A few minutes pass. Lily leans closer to me, her finger hovering over the camera. "Shall I…"

"Yes, please," I reply, watching as another picture appears on-screen. "I can take over from here."

She laughs. "Of course."

With each picture, my body warms with the attention to detail that she's given my first completed work. Is this how everyone sees it? I doubt it. And yet, my eyes grow wet at the thought that I never got to see *The Lovers* in person after it was placed on campus.

I clear my throat. "Have you ever thought of taking pictures of something other than my work?"

A confused look crosses her face. "No. Why?"

"Because your eye for detail is amazing. Instead of just taking pictures of my sculpture in its entirety, you focus close up on the face, the hem of her dress, the little things that many people wouldn't even think to consider."

Her face grows pink. "I don't know what to say. Coming from you, that's a huge compliment. Thank you."

"I'm serious. For example, what would you take a picture of in this room?"

Lily's head pivots back and forth, landing on the French doors. "I suppose the doors and how the light comes through the windows."

I gently hand the camera back to her. "Well then, go ahead."

I watch her as she rises from the sofa. Standing a few inches from the glass, she aims the lens and shoots, the whirring sound reaching back to me. She stops and looks at the screen, no doubt going over what she's captured.

When she returns to me, she hands me the Nikon once more. I examine what she's taken and I gasp in awe

"Lily, the way you captured the sunlight coming through the glass, and then shifted to the sculpture in the back yard...I'm just blown away. You need to take more pictures and start putting together a portfolio."

Her eyebrows rise in shock and her eyes widen. "Seriously?"

I laugh at her reaction. "Yes, seriously. I may not be a photographer, but I am an artist. I have an artist's eye and I know talent when I see it."

"But what do I take pictures of?"

"Anything that inspires you. Make sure you have your camera with you at all times because you never know when inspiration can strike."

She stares at the camera in my hands, a wide smile appearing across her lips. "Okay, I will," she whispers. "Thank you, Grayson. To hear you say all that...It means everything to me because you see something in me that nobody ever has before, not even me."

I tilt my head at her curiously. "You're welcome, Lily."

As she stretches across to take the Nikon from me, the sleeve on her left arm pulls back slightly, and that's when I see an ugly, nasty purple bruise on her wrist. When I examine it closely, it looks as if someone's left fingerprints where the discoloration lies.

Lily must see me staring, because she swiftly pulls her sleeve over the bruise.

I watch her bottom lip trembling now—from fear, embarrassment...I don't know.

"What happened?" I demand.

"N-nothing...I just fell, that's all," she stammers. "I...I should go vacuum upstairs. Thank you again."

Before I can ask her further about the bruise, she flies out of the room.

I sit in silence on the sofa to absorb everything that's just happened. I eventually go back to my studio, but I can't work. I pace mindlessly, then stop at one of the tables, gripping the counter tightly.

I saw it. She probably even forgot it was there.

Who did that to her?

I rush over to my stereo. Nothing classical today. I turn up Hendrix as loud as possible and start to pound clay, working so intensely that I don't even notice when it turns dark outside.

Chapter Nine

Two days later, it's December 24th, and I leave the house with a list of last minute errands as long as my arm.

My arm. Shit, I can't believe I let Grayson see my bruise. I was so humiliated. Thank God I left so quickly. But what he said about taking more pictures and having talent...I can't help but smile.

I wipe everything from my mind because I have a million other things to focus on today.

My first stop is across the river in Catskill, to pick up the centerpiece for my mom's Christmas table.

Walking into the flower shop I'm inundated with the most fragrant scents, ranging from freshly cut pine to bouquets of roses in every color.

Suddenly a pair of small arms envelops me from behind. "*Hola*, Miss Lily!"

I turn around and look down to see Esperanza Rojas's soft brown eyes staring back at me.

"Esperanza, my goodness! What are you doing here?"

She beams back at me with pride. "*Mami* works here sometimes to help out our neighbor."

"*Querida*, let go of Miss Lily," a voice gently admonishes her

When I turn around, Mrs. Rojas is standing behind the counter, holding a poinsettia in her hands.

"My neighbor owns the store, so I always help her out during the holidays. Let me get your order for you from the back. It's all ready to go."

"It's totally fine, Mrs. Rojas. Esperanza can keep me company."

I turn my attention back to Esperanza, who's now biting her lower lip with a worried look on her face.

I touch her shoulder. "What is it, sweetheart?"

She looks down at the floor before reverting her focus back to me. "Thank you for being nice to *Mami*. She told me about the party."

My heart warms at her gratitude. "Of course. I like your mother very much. She's a very nice lady."

The little girl nods her vigorously. "Yes, she is. But she says your boyfriend wasn't very nice. She said he was very mean to you."

My heart rate starts to increase, pounding inside my chest.

Got to love how kids have zero filter.

I swallow and gently squeeze her shoulder to reassure her. "Esperanza, it's okay. He was just very stressed and said some things he shouldn't have. I'm really fine. It was nothing."

Her brown eyes narrow at me, roaming over my face as if she's checking for any sign that I'm not being truthful. "Okay, miss. If you say so."

At that moment, Mrs. Rojas appears from the back carrying my order, a small bouquet of red roses with a white candle sticking up in the center. "That's lovely," I exclaim.

I walk the few steps to the counter to pay. Once I put away my wallet, I take the box in my hands. "Thank you so much, Señora Rojas. Have a lovely Christmas."

"*Gracias*, Miss Moore. *Feliz Navidad!*"

Esperanza races to the door. "I'll get it for you, Miss Lily!" she offers excitedly.

I make my way over to her, but before I can leave she grabs my waist in a quick embrace. "Bye, Miss Lily! *Feliz Navidad!*"

I smile to myself, looking back at Mrs. Rojas for some guidance.

"*Ay*, Esperanza! Let Miss Lily go!"

"Okay, okay," she answers her mother. She releases me and pulls the door open.

I look down at her and give her a full smile. "*Gracias*, sweetheart. *Feliz Navidad!*"

When I reach Ingrid, I put the centerpiece on the floor next to me on the passenger side. I pull out my phone to check my list for my next errand.

Crossing the Hudson River back to Cottage Grove, Esperanza's words swirl around in my head, unsettling me with thoughts of how a child possibly knows me better than I do.

* * *

"Please be nice to her."

"I'm always nice, babe."

"Civil. You're civil. There's a difference."

Taking one hand off the steering wheel, Reed takes my hand in his, bringing it to his mouth and brushing his lips against it. "I swear, Lily, you have nothing to be nervous about."

I nod my head in silence, staring down at the flowers in my lap. I breathe in their scent, not just because they're beautiful but also as a means of calming my nerves.

Ever since Reed and I have been together we've switched our visits between families on Thanksgiving, but for Christmas, it's always the same—Christmas Eve on our own, Christmas Day with my mom, and the 26th (or Boxing Day as Reed's WASP parents refer to it) with Reed's family.

I glance back over at Reed, whose face has a shit-eating grin on it.

"Okay, give it up."

"What?" he asks innocently.

"Something is going on. I've never seen you look this happy when we go to my mom's, especially for Christmas."

"Can't I just be happy? It's Christmas!" he replies a bit too cheerfully.

Next thing I know, he's going to break into song.

Oh yeah, something is definitely up with him.

Thankfully, we finally pull into my mom's driveway behind her Jeep.

Before I can reach for the handle, Reed jumps out and opens the door for me. He takes the centerpiece from me with one hand, helping me from the car with the other.

I give him a smile, even though I'm still suspicious about his good mood and the reason for it. "Thank you."

He leans over and pecks me on the lips. "My pleasure."

I grab my mom's Christmas present from the back seat. Then, taking my hand once more, Reed walks with me up the path to the front door. When I push it open, the scent of roast duck and baked apples and the sound of Elvis singing "Blue Christmas" welcomes us in.

"Mom, we're here!" I shout out into the open space.

Dressed in a jade green knit dress that perfectly matches her eyes, my mother appears from the kitchen.

"Merry Christmas, sweetheart," she greets me with a tight embrace. Releasing me, she turns to Reed. "Hello, Reed. Merry Christmas," Mom says with a modicum of kindness, leaning in to him, giving him a short hug and a swift kiss on his cheek.

"Thank you, Mrs. Moore. I'm glad to be here. I'll just go put this on the table," Reed offers with a smile, gesturing to the flowers in his hands.

"Yes, please. Thank you, Reed," Mom replies. But before I can follow him to the dining room, she grabs me by the elbow.

"What the hell?" she whispers under her breath, her eyes averting to the other room where Reed is now.

I shrug my shoulders. "Your guess is as good as mine. Something is up with him, Mom. I haven't seen him this happy in a long time. It's really freaking me out."

"Me too. Usually he can barely muster a grin. He's never friendly like this; more like civil."

I slap my mother's arm. "Oh my God! I told him that exact same thing in the car on our way over. He said he'd be nice, but almost as if there was more to it."

Mom nods. "I'm getting that." She glances into the kitchen.

"We'd better go join him or he'll start wondering what happened to us. I'll get the hors d'oeuvres and meet you in the living room."

"Good idea," I reply, heading for the living room with the shopping bag holding Mom's present.

My heart grows full when I see the trimmed tree lit up with white twinkle lights. The ornaments I made as a kid, like the clothespin toy soldier and an egg decorated like Santa Claus with a cotton beard and red construction paper hat, are proudly displayed. I gently place Mom's present on the canopy under the tree, already spotting a few brightly wrapped gifts with my name on them.

Mom comes out of the kitchen with a silver tray of cheese and crackers, nearly bumping into Reed coming in from the dining room. "Whoa! Watch out! Where's the fire?"

"Sorry, Mrs. Moore! I'll be right back!" he shouts back over his shoulder.

I stand frozen in place with my mouth hanging open. "Where's he going?" Mom asks as the door slams behind him.

I shake my head. "I have no idea."

A few seconds later he returns, out of breath and carrying a bottle of champagne in his hand. My brows narrow in confusion. "Reed, what's going on?"

He puts the champagne on the coffee table on top of a coaster, then takes a few steps to me, guiding us to the fireplace. "Mrs. Moore, before you go back to the kitchen, I need a moment of your time."

Her eyes give him a quizzical look. "All right."

I exchange glances with Mom when Reed clears his throat. He takes my hands into both of his, looking straight at me.

"Lily, I know I haven't been the best boyfriend lately, and I'm sorry for that. You mean the world to me and I love you. I want to give you a symbol of my love for you, and I hope it'll be with your mother's blessing."

Blessing.

Oh my God…

My hands start to shake.

He can't possibly be…

But he is, because before I can say something, Reed lowers himself to the ground, leaving one knee up as he searches for something in his jacket pocket.

Fuck.

A robin's egg-blue ring box appears in his right hand.

Tiffany.

He pops the top open on the box, revealing the shiniest diamond ring I've ever seen in my life. The stone is round with tiny diamonds lining the band.

"Lily Moore, will you marry me?"

My limbs freeze. Suddenly I've lost all train of thought.

"Baby?"

Reed's quiet yet insistent voice brings me back to where I'm standing, in my childhood home where the man I've dated and lived with for two years has just asked me to marry him.

"Um, Lily, I asked you a question," he laughs nervously.

When I spot Mom sitting on the sofa, her face holds a slight smile. There are tears in her eyes. She doesn't say a word.

"Wh…"

"Lily? My knee's starting to give out."

I take a deep breath. "Okay."

"Yes!" Reed shouts, placing the ring on my finger, then scooping me up into his arms. "Thank God! I thought you were going to say no!"

He puts me down, then holding my hand turns to Mom. "I hope we have your blessing, Mrs. Moore."

She rises from the couch, wiping her eyes before hugging him. "Of course you do, Reed. Congratulations," she replies barely above a whisper, her eyes boring into me. "Reed, would you mind terribly if I had a word with Lily?"

"Oh sure, of course! I'm going to call my parents and tell them the good news."

She watches Reed head into the kitchen, then tugs me over to the side, her face inches from mine. "What were you going to say?"

"What do you mean?"

"Before you said 'okay,' you were going to say something else."

"No I wasn't," I insist.

"Lily. Tell me."

I know better than to hide anything from my mother.

I exhale a breath. "I was going to say 'Why?'"

Mom shakes her head. "I knew it. Why didn't you?"

"Because it would've ruined the moment."

Mom throws her hands up in the air. "Damn it, Lily! Who gives a fuck about the moment? If you had doubts, you should've said something."

Tears begin to flow down my cheeks. "He obviously loves me, Mom. He's trying. Please don't ruin this for me."

Mom rubs her thumbs across my face to wipe away the moisture. "Sweetheart, I just want you to be happy. I don't want you to get hurt."

Reed's voice calls from the kitchen. "Lily! Come here! My parents want to congratulate both of us."

I lean over and kiss Mom on the cheek. "I'll be fine." I rise from the sofa, reaching over to the box of tissues on the coffee table. "Coming!" I reply to my fiancé, wiping away the rest of my tears.

Chapter Ten

I glance around at the gilded dining room of a country club in Saratoga where I'm sitting with my boyfriend (now fiancé) Reed and his parents. Wine glasses clink against each other ever so gently, conversations buoy to the ceiling lilting with laughter and a general feeling of gaiety. The finest cuisine has been consumed, an empty champagne bottle sits abandoned on the damask-covered table.

But for me, the air in the room is stuffy. I pull at the lace collar on my dress as if it were choking me—carefully, so as not to attract any attention to the fact that I'm uncomfortable. I'm here discussing wedding plans with Reed and my future in-laws. I keep reminding myself this is supposed to be a happy occasion. I know Mr. and Mrs. Shepard are doing this to be nice. Maybe I haven't given them the benefit of the doubt all this time. Maybe they are genuinely good people.

I look up to the chandeliers hanging from the ceiling.

I love how the outside light reflects in the crystals. I wish I had my Nikon.

A fingertip taps the top of my hand, interrupting my thoughts. "Lily, my dear, I know a wonderful designer who can create the most beautiful dress for you," his mother says.

"Yes, but I can't afford—"

"You're going to be family, my daughter-in-law, and we simply can't have you walking down the aisle in some off-the-rack frock. Speaking of which, who do you think will be escorting you to the altar?"

Good question, Adeline.

Mrs. Shepard's voice fades in the background as I tune her out.

I can't even comprehend how quickly Reed's parents have adjusted to their heir apparent son marrying a girl who's never belonged to the Junior League or Daughters of the American Revolution. They seem so accepting of the engagement. Did Reed talk to them before he proposed? Give them a Power-Point presentation…

"Mom, Dad, as you can see from the agenda, I've broken down this meeting, 'The Pros and Cons of Marrying Lily Moore', into several categories—physical appearance, job status, financials, potential as mother and wife in a socially prominent family, social liabilities, prenup requirements…"

It might not have happened like that, but something akin to it is a strong possibility.

The sound of Mr. Shepard's patrician voice gets my attention. "Son, I've been thinking. I know you don't have a PhD, but maybe you could get ahead in your job by showing how dedicated you are to it. Like some kind of form of 'extra credit.'"

"I was thinking the same thing," Reed replies. "In fact, I have a meeting this week with the new chair of my department, Tabitha Cross."

"Well done, son. Now you're thinking like a Shepard."

As Adeline drones on and Reed and his father exchange invisible high-fives, my purse vibrates in my lap. I reach in for my phone and see Sky's name on my caller ID.

I slide my chair back before even saying anything, holding the phone up in my hand. "Excuse me, I have to take this."

"Of course, dear."

I look over at Reed, who's engaged in conversation with his father and two men who've stopped by the table, not even noticing that I'm leaving.

I hurry out to a quiet corner in the lobby, bringing the phone to my ear. "Hey, Sky."

"You're *engaged* and I have to hear about it from your mom? I thought I was your best friend."

My shoulders slack in exasperation. "Oh my God. I so sorry I didn't tell you. It's just the past forty-eight hours have been so crazy, and now I'm stuck at some fancy country club with Reed and his parents and his mom is going on and on about wedding dresses…"

"Stop, Lil! Stop! I can hear it in your voice."

I hear her take a breath.

"Look, you know I love you, but I'm really concerned because the last time I saw you you weren't all that gung-ho about Reed, and now you're going to marry him? I just have three words for you."

"And they would be?"

"What the fuck?"

I shake my head. "I know. Could we get together next week for coffee or something? I really need to talk to someone about this."

"Of course we can, sweets. I have to check my teaching schedule. Can I let you know?"

"Absolutely. And thanks."

"That's what besties are for, hon."

I hit end on my phone, inhaling deeply before heading back into the lion's den.

* * *

GRAYSON

I look out the window. A cloudless blue sky stares back at me. I walk over to my closet, sorting through the shirts hanging from the rack to find the perfect one to wear.

Lily will be here today.

I haven't seen her since before Christmas. But now it's the 28th, and she's due back at work today.

I've missed her. I didn't even realize how much until now. It's the way her eyes set ablaze when she gets upset about something. Her self-confidence. How she's never afraid to be honest with me when I'm being a bastard.

I pull on my best pair of freshly washed jeans, followed by the boots I wear in the studio, which are covered in bits of hardened clay.

I check myself out. I look good. Not stuffy, casual bohemian.

Wait.

What the fuck is "casual bohemian"?

I shake my head.

What have I become? Worrying over what I wear just to impress a woman?

I can't let myself do that. It would raise my expectations. Make me hope for the impossible.

I head downstairs from my bedroom. Turning the corner into the kitchen, I hear a commotion in the supply closet. Its door is already slightly ajar, and when I look inside, I see Lily kneeling on the floor, moving the mops in the bucket aside so she can reach the rags in a plastic container under the counter.

I gently whisper her name. "Lily."

Her head bolts up, hitting the wood of the counter above.

"Ow!" she yells in pain.

Oh no.

I reach for her to help her to her feet as she eases out from under the counter. "Oh my God. I'm so sorry. I didn't mean to scare you."

She instantly begins rubbing her head as she stands upright. I'm still holding her elbow to keep her steady.

"It's okay," she says, wincing. "I'm fine."

"How was your Christmas?"

She pauses. "Umm…quiet. Uneventful."

I notice she continues to rub her head.

"Are you sure you're all right?"

She steps back from me. "Yes, yes. It's really okay."

I take a step closer, stretching out my right hand to touch the top of her head. "Please, allow me to check for any bumps to ensure I've caused no injuries."

I hear her let out a slight laugh, still rubbing her head. "Why? You afraid I'm going to sue you or something?"

"What? No, of course not. I just…"

Finally she looks straight at me with a smile. "Grayson, I was joking. I'm fine."

I'm about to answer when our hands touch without warning. My eyes lock on hers. A silence comes over us. All the air has escaped my lungs. I can't look away from her.

An unknown amount of time passes before she finally speaks.

"Really, I'll be okay," she tells me, barely above a whisper.

I'm shifting my hand away from hers when my fingers graze something sharp. She must see the quizzical expression on my face because she quickly snatches her hand down to her side.

It was on her left hand.

I can see her swallow, most likely from nerves.

I stand up taller, now boring my eyes into hers even more.

"Your Christmas wasn't that uneventful, was it?"

She looks down at the floor. "No," she manages. Then she lifts her head and her eyes meet mine. "My boyfriend asked me to marry him and I accepted."

My fists clench. "Well then, I suppose I should wish you congratulations. I hope you'll be very happy. I should get to the studio now."

I can hear her begin to utter 'Thank you' over my shoulder, but I'm already inches from the kitchen door.

I rush down the passageway to the studio. My head swirls with thoughts, thoughts that make me want to pound clay until my hands bleed.

I shove the studio door open, slamming it against the wall. I tear off my shirt, buttons scattering like pebbles to the floor.

But when I turn to my work in progress, I can't face it. It

deserves care and patience, something I'm not capable of right now.

I storm over to the unopened boxes of sculpting clay. I start to open one with my bare hands, pulling at the tape with my fingernails, tearing the top of the box with both hands.

How could she possibly marry him? I don't need to meet him in person to know what kind of a bastard he is. Just from what I heard of that phone call alone is enough to know that he does not deserve her.

And her wrist…she said she fell, but I don't believe that for a second when I could clearly see fingerprints on her skin. I can't fathom why she stays with him when he treats her like a punching bag.

I drop my hands to my sides, panting, out of breath. When I bring my hands back up to my face, I find blood trickling from the beds of my scratched palms, the skin there coming undone.

I sigh and head for the sink in the corner. I turn on the water as cold as it will go. I cringe from the icy temperature as the clear liquid soothes my injuries.

I shake off the excess water, running my hands through my hair.

I inhale deeply, turning back to my work.

Work. That is all I have now.

Chapter Eleven

On my way to meet Sky for coffee, I can't stop thinking about everything that happened yesterday. Between dinner with Reed's parents and Grayson's reaction to my engagement ring, my head won't stop spinning.

A flash of red on the side of road ahead attracts my attention. It's a dilapidated barn, its paint peeling in places with roof tiles missing. But I love how the red still manages to stand out against the white snow on the ground.

I pull Ingrid over and shut off the engine. I grab my Nikon from my bag and step out of the car. I take a few steps closer to the barn and zoom in, clicking away. I put the camera down and just take it all in visually, inhaling a deep breath of fresh winter air.

Sad but still so beautiful. What history does that barn hold? Did someone ever keep cows or horses in there? Why was it abandoned?

A cold breeze permeates my skin. I smile to myself and head back to Ingrid.

* * *

"Have you lost your damn mind?"

Ugh.

I stare back at Sky's fiery blue eyes, practically burning my face with her fury.

Sitting in Cottage Grove's local coffee hangout, Java Joint, I take a sip of my chamomile tea. "No, I haven't. But thank you for your support."

"The last time I saw you, you were a mess about Reed, losing your job, getting that cleaning job, and his complete lack of compassion. He was such a jerk. You can't spend the rest of your life with someone like him. He doesn't deserve you, Lil."

I watch as Sky drinks her double-shot espresso. "We're working things out, Sky. He's been much better since then. Much more understanding and patient. But..."

Her eyes suddenly light up as she leans in closer to me. "But what?"

I take a deep breath. "When he first asked me, I hesitated. My mom was there and witnessed the whole thing. She asked me why I hesitated. I told her it was because my reaction was to ask him why."

"Why he was proposing?"

I nod my head silently.

Without warning, she slams her hands on the wooden table, then just as quickly raises her palms upward, gesturing to me. "You see? *That's* why I don't understand why you said yes."

"Because I love him."

Sky shakes her head at me. "Sweets, I love you, you know

that, right? So I hope you understand what I'm going to say next comes from a place of love."

I prepare myself, inhaling deeply. "Okay."

"Dump his sorry ass or I'll do it for you."

I shake my head vehemently. "No. I won't."

She leans in again, this time yelling at me through gritted teeth. "You can't do this, hon. He is going to make you miserable. Giving you a fucking engagement ring isn't going to change him or make things better between the two of you. When he hits fifty and his mid-life crisis kicks in, he's going to buy a Porsche and cheat on you with some bimbo."

I look away from her, anxious to avoid her glare. I can feel her hand move toward mine, grabbing my fingers. I shift my eyes back to her.

"Lily, please. I know you think you can change him, but you can't. I know it'll be hard to let go because you've been together for so long. But it's time to cut the cord. You've grown apart and you need to find the person you truly deserve to be with."

I shut my eyes, trying to stop the stream of tears that start to form in the corners of them.

"Look at me," Sky whispers.

I open my eyes to see her face, warmer, softened.

"Just think about what I said. Okay?"

I nod. "Okay."

"How's the cleaning job going?" she asks, taking a sip of her coffee.

"Okay. But you won't believe this. It turns out the guy who owns the house is Grayson Shaw."

Her eyes widen in shock. "Wait a sec! The sculptor you like?

The one whose sculpture you're always taking pictures of on campus?"

I nod. "Yup. That's him."

Sky leans into the table. "What's he like?"

"Brooding. Intense. Typical artist. But he can also be sweet. Unfortunately, we didn't exactly have a meet-cute the first time we were introduced."

"What happened?"

"I walked into his studio without asking when he was working, and he scared me off. I wasn't expecting..."

"What?"

I shut my eyes at the memory. "He's got scars on most of his face."

Sky gasps. "From what?"

"His parents died in a car crash when he was a little boy. And he was in the car when it happened."

"That's awful."

"I know. But after I apologized and explained everything to him, he's been much nicer. He's even encouraged me to try my hand at photography. I showed him the pictures I took of his sculpture, and he thinks I have talent; go figure. Weird, huh?"

She grins at me. "Right. *Weird*."

I take a sip of my tea. "No, no, no. It's not like that."

Sky shakes her head at me, laughing to herself. "Lily, you can't bullshit me. You've got this soft, dreamy look in your eyes. I have never once seen you look like that when you talk about Reed. There's obviously something about this guy that stirs something up inside you."

Thankfully her phone pings with a text before I can respond.

When she checks it, she starts typing a reply. "Kane's done with work. I told him I'd meet him at his place."

We both shove back from the table, grabbing our bags. Sky comes around to my side for a tight hug.

"Just think about what I said, okay?"

"Promise."

"I love you, darlin'. Don't forget it."

I smile to myself. "Never do. Never will."

Stepping outside, I give her a wave as she heads to her car. Once she drives away, I walk down a few doors to Cottage Grove Camera Shop in the heart of town. The shop should've closed long ago with the advent of digital, but because so many artists and photographers live in the area it still has a thriving business.

I grab my Nikon from my tote bag and bring it inside.

"Hey, Lily. How's it going?" Matt, the shop owner's nephew, greets me.

"Hi, Matt. I'm good. I need some help."

"Anything you need."

"I want to print out my pictures and I don't have the right kind of printer at home. I need them to look professional because I'm thinking of putting together a portfolio."

"Really? I think that's awesome. All the years you've been coming here, you've never shown an interest in turning professional."

"I know. Let's just say I'm on a path of self-discovery."

"Well, whoever got you into this, I think it's cool as fuck."

I can't help but smile. "Thanks."

And thank you, Grayson.

"Since you're one of our best customers, I'll give you a 20 percent discount on your first set of prints and the portfolio."

I shake my head. "No, really; you don't have to."

"It's done. And when you become rich and famous like Annie Leibovitz, I can tell people I knew you when."

"Ha! If only."

"Trust me. It'll happen. The portfolios are in the back. Pick one out, then you can show me which pictures you want printed."

"Thanks, Matt."

After spending half an hour in the shop, portfolio bought and pictures selected, I walk outside. I'm throwing the hood of my winter jacket over my head when I hear a woman's husky laugh accompanied by a male one.

I turn to my left, spotting Reed walking out of Cottage, the local bistro, with a tall, lithe woman who I immediately recognize as Tabitha Cross, the head of the computer science department.

I quickly duck back into the doorway of the shop before they can spot me.

I watch as she throws a fur wrap over her shoulders, flipping her long, silky dark brown hair. She gives another throaty laugh, gently touching Reed's arm with her hand. They stand within inches of each other when Tabitha suddenly leans into him to whisper something into his ear.

He smiles in return, and it's not a smile best friends give to each other. This smile has meaning, intent, and promise. I should know because I had that smile aimed at me when Reed and I were first dating.

My heart drops when she gives him a soft brush of her lips across his cheek, and his right arm comes around her to bring her in closer.

I don't know whether to cry or confront them, to tear that wrap from around her skinny shoulders.

With his hand on the small of her back, Reed leads her to a British racing green Jaguar, opening the door for her, giving her a peck on the cheek before she settles into the driver's seat. He watches as she reverses out of the space, then walks down the street to his BMW.

Taking deep breaths, I fight the silent tears that fall from my eyes. I wipe my face clean with my glove, slowly making my way back to Ingrid. I give her a hipcheck and open the door. With shaking hands, I insert the key into the ignition, but I can't move beyond that. I grip the steering wheel, knowing it won't break under my hold because I need something on which to take out my anger and my heartbreak, and let the tears flow freely.

Driving home, thoughts of Grayson fill my mind. I wonder what he's doing now. Is he working in his studio dressed only in those jeans he was wearing the first time I saw him? Is he resting after a long day creating something beautiful? Is he discussing future showings with Emilia?

I shake my head, gripping the steering wheel harder.

Why the hell am I thinking about him at this exact moment?

By the time I get home, Reed's car is already in the driveway, covered by its ever-present tarp. When I walk in, he's standing in the foyer, sorting through the mail.

I wipe my feet on the mat, reaching over to greet him with a quick kiss. "Hi."

"Hey," he replies, clearly distracted by the bounty of men's clothing catalogs he's received.

"Where were you just now? I could've sworn I saw you in town."

I observe his face carefully to see if he'll reveal anything.

Nothing. No twitch or flinch.

"Nope. I had a faculty meeting on campus."

"You're a liar, Reed. I just saw you in town with Tabitha Cross, your boss. Care to explain that?"

He sighs audibly. "Fine. If you must know, Tabitha took me out to lunch because she felt badly."

"Badly about what?"

"My observation. It was a clusterfuck. Everything that could've gone wrong did. So she was trying to console me."

My shoulders drop. "Reed, I'm sorry about your observation. I really am. But you have to understand where I'm coming from. You're my fiancé, so when I see you with another woman, of course I'm going to get suspicious."

"Lily, we're fucking engaged. That says a lot right there."

Not enough.

I take a deep breath. "Why are you with me?"

He looks up from the mail, pivoting his head to me. "What kind of question is that?"

I let my purse and tote fall to the floor. "I'm serious, Reed. I want to know why you're with me."

"Because we're perfect for each other. Everyone knows it."

My eyebrows narrow, and I'm desperate to know the answer to my next question. "Who's everyone?"

"The people I work with, my parents, my friends."

"Do you even like me?"

He puts down the mail on the sideboard, taking my face in his hands and kissing me lightly on the lips. "I love you. You keep me grounded. You make me want to be a better man. And you're beautiful, exactly what I want my wife to be."

I return his kiss, now thoroughly confused by those last words.

He didn't say, "You're beautiful inside and out." It's only the external beauty he was talking about.

I pull back a good foot away from him. "So, you think I'm physically attractive, and that's your number one criteria for a wife?"

His eyes widen at my question. "What the hell? Of course not."

"Well, that's what you're implying."

"You're just reading between the lines. So typical."

I shake my head.

Unbelievable.

"Fuck, Reed! I am so tired of your bullshit. One minute you're so sweet, giving me gifts, and the next minute you turn cold and cruel. I defend you constantly to my mom, telling her that you're really a good person deep down, but then you say shit like that, that having a beautiful wife is what matters to you."

"I didn't—"

He needs to stop talking.

I hold up my right hand to him, palm facing out. "You know what? I think we need a break."

His eyes light up in fury. "What?"

"We need this, Reed. I'm going to stay with my mom for a while until we can figure things out."

He lets out a deep breath, waving his hand dismissively at me. "Fine. I'm sick of arguing all the time, too."

I rush upstairs and pack a duffel bag with extra clothes. On my way out, I find him sitting on the sofa, skimming through a catalog.

"I'll come by once a day to get the mail."

He shrugs his shoulders. "It's your house, too, Lily."

I pick up my bag from the floor. "Call if you need anything."

He nods without looking up at me.

Thanks, honey. I can just feel the love.

When I pull into my mom's driveway, she's already standing in the doorway.

She watches in silence as I walk up to the house, duffel in hand. Once she shuts the door behind me, my mom gives me one of the tightest hugs ever.

"Go sit down. I'll get you some tea," she whispers in my ear.

I take off my boots and collapse into the soft cushions of the couch in the living room. An old black and white movie is playing on the TV screen.

Mom comes back into the room, carefully placing a steaming mug of tea on a coaster in front of me on the coffee table.

She settles in next to me. "Tell me."

I sigh, leaning back. "I just had enough, Mom. Arguing all the time. I told him we needed a break, so I'm here."

Oh yeah, and I also saw him with another woman, but that's not something I care to share with you at this particular moment.

"Well, I'm not going to say it…"

"Restrain yourself, Mother."

She laughs at loud. "I will. I'm here for you no matter what."

I lean over and kiss her on the cheek, grabbing her tightly. "Thanks, Mom."

When I pull back from her, I reach for my tea, blowing off the steam.

"So, how's the job going?"

I put down the mug. "It's actually going pretty well. You won't believe who owns the house."

"Who?"

"Grayson Shaw."

Mom's eyes widen in surprise. "You're kidding. Wow. He's that sculptor you like, right? I can't believe it. It's as if you were meant to get that job."

I shake my head in disbelief. "I know."

She curls her legs under her. "Tell me. What's he like?"

I purse my lips in contemplation. "He's very overwhelming at first, kind of like a hulking beast. He gets angry easily, but it doesn't bother me because he's a recluse. He never leaves his house, so he never interacts with anyone, only Emilia, the woman who runs his affairs for him. But he can be so kind sometimes. He just doesn't show it that often."

When I finish describing him, my mother's eyebrows are narrowed in confusion, which is freaking me out.

"What?"

"I'm not exactly thrilled at the idea of my only child working for a man who can't control his temper."

"He's really not that bad, Mom. He's nothing like Reed."

Now a slight smile crosses her face.

I sigh in exasperation. "Okay, now you're confusing the hell out of me. Why are you smiling?"

"Call me crazy, but you've never talked about Reed with a dreamy look in your eyes or this sweet smile plastered on your face. If this is what he's like and makes my kid light up like a damn Christmas tree, then I'm all for it."

"That's what Sky said," I mutter to myself under my breath.

"What?"

I peck her on the cheek to distract her. "You *are* crazy, Mom."

She gives me a knowing grin and stands up, kissing me lightly on the forehead. "I'll go make up your bed, honey. Just think about what I said."

Five hours later, lying in bed wide awake, my mother's words are still echoing in my head.

Thanks a lot, Mom.

* * *

GRAYSON

What is Lily doing now?

I watch the first snowflakes fall to the ground from my bedroom window. Another flurry approaches. I hope the roads will be passable so she can make it in safely tomorrow.

I miss her face.

I miss her voice, especially when she's dressing me down.

She always seems to have a positive outlook on life. What I wouldn't give for an iota of that.

I check the antique grandfather clock in my bedroom.

Nearly midnight.

Almost tomorrow.

I will see her soon.

Chapter Twelve

The smell of roasted beef invades my nose when I enter Grayson's house the next morning.

A tray of steaming food sits on the kitchen counter. Emilia is rushing around, putting on her coat while grabbing a piece of paper from a magnetic notepad on the fridge.

She turns around and sees me, her shoulders dropping in relief. "Oh, thank God you're here. I'm so late for a doctor's appointment and I had to get Grayson's lunch tray ready. I need you to take it to him, all right? I'll be back in a few hours. You can go home after you give it to him. I checked over everything, and there's nothing that needs to be done."

"But what—"

Before I can even manage to finish my question, Emilia flies past me out the front door.

I stare at the tray, knowing I should get it out to him before it gets cold.

Leaving my purse on the counter, I heave the tray into my

hands. Approaching the door leading to the passageway, I realize I need to open it first before walking through with the tray.

I look out, finding a well-lit concrete tunnel. The hallway is wide and long, with a side table to the right just inside the doorway.

I pick up the tray and carefully walk it through, laying it down on the table. I shut the door firmly behind me. My steps echo down the hallway, wondering if he can hear me approaching.

I reach the end of the way, managing to hold onto the tray while giving two hard knocks to the wood door before me.

The door swings open, revealing Grayson. He's wearing a white T-shirt covered in streaks of clay and torn jeans, and his feet are bare. His brown eyes turn soft and widen at the sight of me.

"Oh, hello. I was expecting Emilia."

"She asked me to bring your lunch. She was running late for a doctor's appointment."

His eyebrows rise. "Of course. I completely forgot. Please come in."

I step into the studio cautiously. I can see the next sculpture he's working on. Something short and standing on a pedestal.

"Lily."

I shake my head. "Forgive me. I was just looking at what you're working on now."

"I'd rather you didn't."

I avert my eyes from the clay. "I'm sorry."

"No harm done," he reassures me. "I'm just very sensitive about my work. You can put the tray down on the desk."

I do as he says. "Speaking of work, how is your portfolio coming along?" he asks with my back to him.

I spin around. "It's coming along slowly, but I'm enjoying myself."

He smiles at me. "That's wonderful. You wouldn't by chance have your portfolio with you?"

My body warms from his question. I can't stop grinning. "I do, actually. It's in my car."

"I'd love to see it after I finish lunch."

"You can call me on the house phone when you're finished and—"

He waves his hand at me. "No, no. Don't be silly. I'll bring the tray in myself. You can show it to me then."

I nod. "Okay. I'll get it from my car in the meantime."

I reach the door, my hand on the doorknob, when a thought strikes me.

When I turn around to face him, he's sitting at his desk, about to tuck into the meal.

"Grayson, may I ask you a question? You don't have to answer if you don't want to."

He looks at me curiously. "Go on."

"Have you…do you…I mean…"

"Just ask, Lily."

"Do you need more than art to make you happy?"

"I'm perfectly content with my life."

"'Content' isn't the same as happy. I understand what you mean, but hiding away in your studio on this crumbling estate doesn't exactly help you," I counter.

I dare myself to look directly at Grayson, fearing the fury I expect to see in his eyes. Instead, a flash of amusement crosses his face. "Come again?"

My tongue tangles in my mouth as I attempt to form something more mature to say. "I…I…oh, hell." I stop short when a deep laugh rumbles from his throat. My eyes widen in surprise.

He lifts his hand to me, palm facing out. "Continue, please."

My shoulders relax from the amused sound of his voice. I clear my throat. "I meant to say that you need to open up to people and learn to trust them if you ever want something good to happen in your life. Surely you need more than your art to make you happy."

I shut my eyes.

Too far. I went too far.

When I open my eyes again, he is standing over me. My heart starts pounding inside my chest as his eyes sear into me. He remains resolutely silent.

Leave. Move your damn feet. Leave now.

"I should go. Eat before it gets cold. I'll go get my portfolio."

I rush out the door, not even thinking once of looking back.

Once I reach the kitchen, I grip the counter to calm myself, shaking my head.

Fuck. Why did I say all that? I have no right…

The sound of my cell ringing in my pocket jolts me from my thoughts. Reed's name is on the caller ID.

"Hi. Everything okay?" I ask.

"Yeah. Look, I know we're taking a break, but I had an idea."

I can't help but be curious. "What?"

"I thought maybe we could recreate where we first met, our date, something like that."

I pause, wondering if he's being sincere.

"Look, I know I've been a complete shit to you, and I think we need to remind ourselves why we fell in love in the first place."

Before I can say something, he stops me. "Lily, I miss you and I love you."

My eyes shut from the power of his words.

Oh, fuck it. I need to try.

"Okay."

"I'll pick you up tonight at seven."

I nod my head. "I'll see you then."

* * *

GRAYSON

"Surely you need more than your art to make you happy."

That's all I could think about as I ate my lunch, and on the short trek to the kitchen with the tray.

Nobody's ever dared to speak to me like that before. But then, she was right. Nobody could speak to me like that because I've never left my crumbling estate. She was right about that, too. It is crumbling because I never cared before if the walls of my home fell around me. Who would care?

When I enter the kitchen carrying the tray, Lily is standing at the sink. She turns to me. "Just bring it over. I'll take care of the dishes while I'm here. My portfolio's on the table."

She looks up at me with a quick grin, then takes the dishes and cutlery from the tray. I throw away my used napkin and put away the tray and salt and pepper shakers.

On the table is a zippered black leather portfolio. I sit down and slowly unzip the binder. Behind me, the water at the sink stops running, and a minute later Lily settles next to me.

I open the portfolio, coming face to face with the first picture—a close-up of the woman in *The Lovers*.

"I took more," she says nervously.

I smile back at her. "Don't worry. I believe you."

And she did, because the next set of photos is of an old red barn standing in the snow.

I gasp in wonder. "Wow. That's beautiful. I love the contrast between the red and white."

"Thank you. I can't explain it, but for some reason I'm drawn to contrasting colors."

"That's what you should name your first showing: 'Contrast.'"

"Yeah, right."

I glance at her, her eyes rolling at me. "'My first showing.' Are you kidding? I'm just starting out."

"I'm not saying it'll happen next week, but if you keep at it, you'll never know what is truly possible until you believe in yourself and your craft."

Her eyebrows narrow at me. "You're not joking, are you?"

"No. Don't you think you can do this? Have you shared this with anyone else?"

"Just my best friend Sky. And Matt at the camera shop."

"Yes, of course. Matt at the camera shop." She laughs at my teasing, warming my heart when I hear her reaction. I keep turning the pages, astounded by her talent. "But what about your fiancé?" I ask her.

I look up when she doesn't reply right away. Her smile has disappeared. "I could never tell him. He wouldn't understand. He's not exactly the creative type."

"That's too bad. He's your fiancé, after all."

She nods silently. "I'd better go. I have some chores to finish."

As she reaches for the portfolio, my hand brushes her warm one. Our eyes instantly lock on each other, neither of us speaking, our chests rising and falling with each breath. Her soft lips form an O as if she's expecting something to happen.

I finally break the silence. "Thank you for showing it to me."

She nods. "Of course. You're welcome."

Just as she's about to walk away, I call out her name. She turns around to face me.

"You can do this, Lily. Don't stop pursuing what you love. I believe in you."

She freezes at my words. I open my mouth to say something but her voice stops me. "Thank you, Grayson," she whispers.

I watch her leave, standing still, absorbing her gratitude, her calm demeanor, her innocence.

When I return to the studio, I get to work, pounding the clay. Again and again.

As much as I try to escape them, her words continue to occupy my mind.

I never leave my home because I fear the outside. To me, the outside is where I lost my parents, how I became the monster I look like today. I fear strangers' reactions to me when they see me in person.

This is where I find peace. Nobody to judge me. It is only me in this wide open space, living my passion, creating something beautiful.

But she's right. About everything. Every goddamn thing.

I do need something more than my art to make me happy. But the one thing I want I can never have.

I put down the clay and walk over to my desk. Opening a drawer, I pull out a clean sheet of vellum stationery and an envelope.

Chapter Thirteen

I *miss you. I love you.*"

I hadn't been able to shake off those words since Reed said them to me, small as they were yet potent with meaning. They became my earworm, all in his voice.

Until...

"*I believe in you.*"

Grayson Shaw, the world famous artist, believes in me and my talent.

Driving home, I know that I could never share any of my art with Reed. I can't bring it up with him tonight. He would laugh in my face, dismiss it as just a hobby.

Could Grayson see me shiver when our hands touched at the table? When we couldn't stop looking at each other?

What was that?

I shake my head to clear all my thoughts as I pull into the driveway.

When I walk in, I see a gorgeous bouquet of pink roses on the kitchen table.

"Who are those from?" I ask Mom. She's standing at the stove stirring something in a deep pot.

"I don't know. They're for you. They were on the stoop when I got home."

I enter the kitchen, taking the card from the bouquet. *Thank you. Reed.*

I pick up the vase, inhaling the intoxicating scent of the roses, a gift from my fiancé.

He's trying, too. Give him another chance.

"Who sent them?"

"Reed."

"Are you serious?"

"Yes, and he's taking me out tonight."

The sound of a metal spoon banging against the counter echoes against the kitchen walls. "Damn it, honey. He doesn't deserve you."

"Mom, please don't give me shit for this. He's trying, so I have to as well. Just be nice when he gets here, okay?"

"What time?"

"Seven."

She mumbles something under her breath as I give her a quick peck on the cheek on my way up to my room to change.

* * *

The doorbell rings promptly at seven that night.

"Sweetpea, Prince Charming is here," my mom shouts up the stairs to me.

I check myself one last time in the mirror—black cowl neck

sweater, jeans, black boots. I grab my purse from the bed and head downstairs.

Mom stands at the bottom of the stairs waiting for me, her eyebrows raised.

"Stand down, Mom. Your disdain is showing."

"This is not a good idea, honey."

"He's my fiancé. I have to at least give him another chance."

She stops shaking her head just as I open the door to let in Reed, who's also wearing a sweater and jeans, holding a single red rose.

He holds it out to me. "Hey," he greets me, leaning in to hug me.

"Thanks. Let me get my coat."

I hand the rose to my mom, who gives me another disapproving look.

"Good evening, Mrs. Moore," he says to my mom.

"Hello, Reed," she replies through gritted teeth.

I retrieve my down jacket from the closet along with my scarf, gloves, and hat. Reed helps me into my coat, holding it for me. With his back to her, he can't see Mom roll her eyes at him.

"Such a gentleman," she mouths silently to me.

I frown at her remark, then just as quickly slap on a smile when I turn back to Reed.

"We won't be too late, Mom," I shout over my shoulder.

"Be safe, please," she answers back just before shutting the door.

Reed comes to my side of the car first, holding the door open for me.

Once we're both buckled in, silence permeates the interior.

We glance at each other, instantly bursting into peals of laughter.

"Why are we so nervous?" I ask him.

He shakes his head. "I don't know. It's not like we've never done this before." He stops laughing. "Ready?"

"Yeah, let's do this. Get ready, Memory Lane."

Reed turns on the satellite radio to a classic rock station. The voice of John Fogerty comes out of the speakers singing "Bad Moon Rising," accompanying us as we travel over the Hudson to the Ashby campus.

Great.

So help me if Creedence Clearwater Revival is trying to tell me something…

I mouth along to the radio's playlist the rest of the way until Reed reaches campus, pulling up in front of his old frat house.

I smile to myself. "You remember."

"Of course I remember. How could I forget? It was rush week freshman year. You were wearing a cute white lacy top with flowers—"

"Which soon turned a light amber color when you bumped into me and spilled beer all over it. It was ruined," I conclude his recollection.

"Yeah, sorry about that. But as I recall, I was very apologetic."

"You were also nervous, trying to get rid of the stain by blotting some wet napkin over it."

He cringes. "Did you know I was just doing that to cop a feel?"

I tilt my head at him. "Reed, I wasn't born yesterday."

"I know, babe. So, next stop…the diner."

He starts the car again and backs out of the space.

Ok, so far, so good.
Give him a chance.

* * *

Hot grease spills down our fingers onto our arms as we bite into the burger deluxe special at the Cottage Grove Diner.

We glance at each other and grin, fighting the urge to laugh so we can swallow our food.

"I was trying to be so ladylike when I ate one of these on our date."

Reed smiles at me. "I gotta give you credit for that. Your burger was spilling everywhere, and you dapped at your mouth so daintily with ketchup and grease all over your chin."

"Not one of my finest moments."

"I did tell you to order anything on the menu."

"And I did. I'm definitely not one of those 'I'll just have a salad' girls. But I'm glad I didn't turn you off with my eating habits."

His eyes grow softer. "Lily, I dated enough of those salad girls before I met you. You completely enchanted me that night."

My shoulders relax at his pronouncement, my entire body warming from his honesty. "That's one of the nicest things you've ever said to me."

"And it won't be the last. So, dessert. Hot fudge brownie sundae for two?"

He remembered.

I nod as I wipe my chin, this time not so daintily. "Let's just try to finish these burgers first."

* * *

"So…"

"So…"

"This is awkward."

"It's definitely like our first date all over again."

We're standing at my mom's front door, staring into each other's eyes. His gloved hands hold mine.

He clears his throat. "Thank you for tonight, Lily. It really meant a lot to me that you agreed to this."

"You're welcome. It meant a lot to me, too. But I can't…"

He nods his head. "I know. I know. I won't push. Just move back in when you're ready. I miss you, that's all."

"I know you do. Baby steps, okay?"

"Okay." He leans in, giving me a short yet soft kiss. "I'll call you."

He's heading to his car when I call out to him. "Hey, Reed."

He turns back around to me. "Yeah?"

"I've been thinking…I'd like to take some classes about photography."

"You mean as a general topic? About famous photographers?"

"No, how to become one. A photographer, that is."

He comes back, stopping a few inches away from me. "Why in the hell would you want to do something like that?"

I hold my head high. "Because I think I'd be good at it."

My fiancé shakes his head at me. "Babe, photography is a hobby, not a profession. Stick to teaching. It's what you're good at." He kisses me quickly on the lips. "We'll talk soon."

He walks back to his car, giving me a wave before he drives away.

I don't wave back.

I told Grayson that my fiancé would laugh at me if I told him about my aspirations to become a photographer. Now I almost wish he had laughed at me. That would've hurt less.

Fuck.

No, on second thought, it would've been just as painful.

I open the front door, shutting it quietly behind me.

"Good. You're home."

My mom's voice startles me; my hand flies to my chest. I turn around to see her standing at the bottom of the stairs in her dark red bathrobe. "I'm glad you're a nurse because I think I just had a heart attack."

"You're such a drama queen. So, did Prince Charming lure you back to his castle?"

"No," I reply without hesitation. "I told him I needed more time, and he said he was okay with that."

She rolls her eyes at me. "I'll believe it when I see it." She takes a step closer to me, reaching out to touch my face. "I just don't want you to get hurt, sweetpea."

I smile at the feel of my mother's touch. "I won't, Mom. And anyway, that's not possible. I'm Joanie Moore's kid."

She pecks me on the cheek, enveloping me in a tight embrace. "Damn straight."

Chapter Fourteen

I sweep the vacuum one last time across the worn carpets on the second floor. I switch off the power and stretch my back, listening to the bones crack in my spine.

Thankfully, Emilia hasn't asked me to do anything for Grayson today. I think I need space from him. I don't like these feelings fluttering inside me like a butterfly, as if they're an indication that I'm harboring some kind of deeper emotions for him. He's the one who signs my paychecks, and besides that, I'm not being fair to Reed. He's been so nice to me, texting and calling frequently to see how I am, taking me out for brunch this past weekend.

I'll tell Reed today. I'm ready to give us a fresh start. Maybe even stop by the store on the way home so I can pick up some things to make a special dinner for him.

I roll the vacuum back into its resting place in the hall closet. When I reach the kitchen, there's a note on the counter.

Lily,

I've gone to town. Mr. Shaw is in his studio. You may leave for the day once you've finished upstairs. Your paycheck is on my desk.

Emilia

I exhale in relief, knowing I can deposit my check on the way home.

I can't help smiling to myself as I drive into town. Everything seems brighter; the center of town is bustling with everyone greeting each other.

As the ATM processes my deposit, the wail of a fire engine screams behind me. When I turn around, I see two trucks from the Cottage Grove Fire Department rush down the street, sirens at full volume.

Several people stop to watch with me.

"What's going on?" a young woman pushing a baby stroller asks aloud, echoing the thoughts of the crowd gathered near me.

An older man approaches us with a bunch of manila envelopes in his hand, probably heading for the post office. "I just drove past Ashby. Huge cloud of smoke over the campus. No clue which building, but that's my guess where they were headed."

Ashby.

Reed.

I sign out of my account, snatch my card and receipt from the machine, and run to Ingrid, tires screeching as I pull out into the street.

I press my foot to the accelerator, breaking the speed limit to campus.

Part of the campus is already cordoned off by yellow tape when I pull into the visitor parking lot. I slam Ingrid shut behind me and run straight toward the source of the smoke.

Fire trucks with the names of Cottage Grove's neighboring towns—Hudson, Claverack, and Chatham—surround a building on the edge of campus. When I realize it's the art studio, I heave a sigh of relief because it's not the building where Reed's office is located.

I come to a stop where campus police barricades have blocked access to the area of the campus closer to the studio. Firemen shout instructions at each other, water shoots into the sky from long hoses over the burning roof of the studio, smoke continues to billow into thick clouds floating up into the sky.

In the distance, a lone figure steps into the light from the fire, doubled over coughing while tugging up his pants. When he rises to standing position, I gasp in shock.

I duck under the barricades and rush to him. "Reed!"

A fireman reaches Reed before I do and brings him to safety. I can tell Reed's saying something to him amid his coughing fits, but he looks in my direction when he hears me call his name again, his eyes widening in surprise.

I grab Reed and tug him roughly into my arms. "Oh my God! Honey, what were you doing in there?"

"I…I was walking by when I saw the smoke," he manages to get out, his chest vibrating against mine from the power of his coughing. "I wanted to be sure there was nobody in there."

I quickly check him over. The buttons on his shirt are out of place, his tie is loosened around his neck, and his hair, usually not one strand out of place, is disheveled.

He wasn't just walking by.

"Why is—"

"You're very brave, kid," the fireman praises him. "Miss, he needs oxygen. We need to get him to the paramedics."

"Oh, of course. Let's—"

Before I can finish my sentence and disentangle from Reed, another firefighter heads in our direction from the burning building, his arm wrapped around a tall woman with dark hair. His jacket covers her shoulders because she's only wearing a red knit dress, with nothing on her feet. When her face comes into focus, I fist the back of Reed's shirt, clenching my hands together in subdued rage.

Tabitha. Reed's colleague.

He was with her in the studio.

He wasn't walking by.

He wasn't being a Good Samaritan.

He was fucking her.

I pull back from Reed, dropping my arms from his body. I can't even speak as I stare at him.

You fucking liar.

When he finally looks into my eyes with curiosity, he doesn't say anything until he hears Tabitha coughing behind him. His eyes close with a wince.

That's right. You're busted, asshole.

Before he can say anything the fireman pulls him from me, leading him to the waiting ambulance, where Tabitha has been brought as well. I stand back to see if they acknowledge each other or interact in any way.

They don't even look at each other.

Oxygen masks are placed over their mouths as I approach them. A young paramedic comes up to me. "Are you any relation?"

I nod in Reed's direction. "He's my fiancé," I mutter under my breath.

"We'll have to take them both to Hudson Community for observation. You can meet us there."

"Fine," I reply through gritted teeth.

Reed and Tabitha climb into the ambulance. I watch as the doors are shut and the vehicle pulls away, its siren screaming.

* * *

When I step into the emergency room, my mom is standing at the front desk, shouting into a phone. "What part of 'urgent' don't you understand?"

She slams the phone down, then looks up and sees me, rushing to me from around the counter. "Sweetpea, how are you doing? Reed is much better, by the way." She comforts me, patting my hair. Then she sniffs it. "Honey, why do you smell like smoke?"

I pull back from her. "Because I was there when Reed came out of the building."

Mom grabs my shoulders. "What? Why were you on campus?"

I sigh. "I was in town depositing my paycheck when the fire engines went by and some guy said there was a fire at Ashby, so I drove over to make sure Reed was safe. When I got there, he came out of the art studio covered in smoke and soot."

A puzzled look crosses her face. "Wait, the fire was in the art studio?"

"Yes," I whisper.

"What the hell was he doing in there?"

Out of the corner of my eye, I see the alleged reason as she steps out from behind the curtain of one of the examination areas, wearing paper slippers on her feet and a warming blanket around her shoulders. She freezes when she sees me. Mom approaches her, as any nurse would.

"Dear, are you well enough to sign out?"

She coughs slightly. "Yes, the doctor said I was fine and to come back if I had any recurring symptoms."

"Good, then let's take care of your paperwork and get you out of here."

"Thank you," she mutters, averting her eyes from me.

Mom turns back to me. "Sweetie, I have to get back to work. You're going to wait for Reed, aren't you?"

He should find his own fucking ride home.

Keep cool. Don't give anything away yet.

"Of course." I reply with a fake grin plastered across my face, watching Tabitha Cross slowly make her way to the counter.

Mom stops for a second to give me a second glance, then leans in for a quick hug. "I'm glad Reed is okay. We'll talk later."

"Yup."

Just as Mom turns away toward the front desk, a young resident in green scrubs approaches me. "Miss Moore?"

"Yes, that's me."

"Your fiancé would like to see you."

My eyebrows furrow. "Where is he?"

"Come with me."

I purse my lips and follow him to one of the partitioned areas. Metal screeches across metal when he pulls back the curtain for me. "He's fine to go home. Just keep an eye on him in case he has any trouble."

I nod in acknowledgment.

Reed doesn't know the meaning of the word 'trouble'…but now he will.

At the sight of me Reed shuts his eyes and inhales deeply, as if he's preparing for the battle to come.

Clenching my fists I step toward him, leaving a few inches between us. "Let me know if you need anything," the resident offers behind me before he pulls the curtain back across the metal rod.

"Lily, let me explain—"

I hold up my hand to his face. "Stop. No, Reed. It's taking all the strength I have not to slap the shit out of you and yell at you so everyone in the ER can hear, even my mother."

"Did you say anything to her?" he asks sheepishly.

I laugh and shake my head. "Do you think your head and your limbs would still be attached to your body if I had?"

He nods his head, realizing how obvious that answer is.

"Of course not," I continue. "I didn't tell her that the poor woman who was brought in with you is the skank you've been fucking behind my back," I snap at him.

"Please, baby, nothing happened," he swears to me, reaching out to touch my arm.

I jerk back from him. "Don't," I warn him. "I don't believe anything you say anymore. I can't do this. We are done, Reed."

"I can change, baby."

I shake my head at him. "That's not in your DNA. If it were, you wouldn't have cheated on me."

Tears form in the corners of his eyes. I press my lips together to keep my own from falling down my cheeks.

This is it. This is the end of us.

I can do this.

I take one step closer to him. His eyes follow my hands as I slowly remove my engagement ring. I take one of his hands, opening the palm and dropping the ring into it. "This is what we're going to do," I begin in a quiet yet strong, unwavering tone. "You're going to pretend that nothing is wrong when we walk out of here. We'll exchange pleasantries with my mother, not giving away the fact that we just broke up for good. I'm going to drive you home and I'm leaving you there. Tomorrow morning, I'll return to pack up as much as I can and move back in permanently with my mother. I'll get the rest of my things while you're at work. Am I clear?"

"Yes," he replies, barely above a whisper.

"Good." I gesture at his feet. "Get your shoes on. I'll wait for you outside."

I turn for the curtain, tugging it open and closing it behind me, never looking back.

Chapter Fifteen

Hmmm. Hmmm. Hmmm.

I catch myself humming as I drive up the hill to Grayson's house the next morning.

I'm *humming*.

I'm not humming any song in particular. It's just...I feel so much lighter. I feel amazing.

Is this what it feels like to be truly independent, to put myself first for a change?

Pulling Ingrid into my usual space at Grayson's house and walking in...I can't stop fucking humming.

In the closet where I put away my coat and purse, there's a white envelope in the same spot where Grayson left the postcard for me.

"Miss Lily Moore" is written across it in perfect calligraphy.

I pick up the letter, going back to the kitchen for a knife. I slowly slide it across the top of the envelope. It would feel awkward opening such a gorgeous envelope with my thumb. Maybe working here is teaching me to appreciate beautiful things and treating them with respect, like how Emilia talked about the silver that I polished.

When I pull out the letter and open it, Grayson's name is engraved across the top—black ink on ivory paper. There is only one sentence written in his hand:

Thank you for sharing your work with me.

I smile to myself and reread the note.

I just…this is just…

"Thank you so much, dear."

I jump in surprise, holding the note close to my chest. When I turn around, Emilia's there, dressed in cashmere sweats and sneakers.

"Oh my God, you scared me! What are you thanking me for?"

"I don't know what happened when you took Grayson's lunch to him, but ever since then, his attitude has completely changed. He actually thanked me for something, and then he hugged me. *Hugged me.* I can't even remember the last time he did that. And I know you're the one responsible for the change in him."

My face heats up from the unexpected praise. "Emilia, I didn't do anything. Really."

She waves her hand at me dismissively. "Think whatever you like, my girl. I know the truth."

I bite my bottom lip. "Do you think he's busy now? I'd like to tell him something."

"Of course. Just knock once, and if he doesn't answer leave him be. I have to go up into the attic to find some documents."

"I wondered why you were dressed so casually."

"Cobwebs, my dear. The bane of my existence."

I laugh at her explanation, taking the route through the French doors at the back of the house to reach his studio instead of the cold tunnel.

I knock once as Emilia instructed, and much to my surprise Grayson opens the door within a minute.

I'm about to speak but Grayson beats me to it. "Good morning, Lily."

I swallow hard because of his attire—more like his *lack* of it.

He's wearing his torn jeans again, the ones he had on when I first knocked on this door. And nothing else.

But now, instead of running off like a frightened little girl like I did that first time, I'm able to take in and appreciate the beauty of his upper body. Every muscle in his chiseled chest and torso is perfectly formed. When he flexes his arms, the corded veins on his forearms stand out against his skin. He is so virile, so present that I have to blink a few times to find my bearings.

Speak slowly. Don't stammer like an idiot.

I take a deep breath. "Good morning, Grayson. I just wanted to thank you for the note. It was very kind of you."

A wide smile crosses his face. "I meant it."

"This seems to be a day for 'thank you.'"

He cocks his head at me curiously. "Pardon?"

I shake my head. "It's nothing." A sudden thought strikes me. "I was thinking it's such a gorgeous day. It's not too cold. Why don't we take a walk in the gardens? I'd love for you—"

His face grows red instantly. "No."

I pull him by his wrist, yanking as hard as I can. "Come on. You probably need a break anyway, so—"

"I said no!" He growls at me so forcefully that I actually take a step back from the fury in his protest.

I stand stunned, silent, still holding onto his arm. He doesn't say a word either. Our eyes lock on each other's. I drop his arm from my grasp.

"I'm sorry I yelled. Forgive me. It's just…"

My heartbeat turns rapid, waiting for him to continue.

"I'm agoraphobic, Lily. I never go outside."

My heart breaks at his admission. "How long have you been like this?"

"Ever since I lost my parents. The outside is where they died, and it's where I'd be judged by my looks."

I tread carefully. "Have you sought treatment for it? Medicine, therapy?"

He shakes his head. "I don't see the point. It would be money wasted."

I slowly reach out to lace his fingers with mine. They are rough and callused, but warm in my grasp. "It wouldn't be a waste. And I would never judge you."

When he finally glances up at me, his eyes have softened. "I'm beginning to see that. But I still can't do it."

Don't push him.

I drop his hand and start to walk away, but then stop when I hear him call my name.

I turn to face him. "What?"

"I'm sorry," he mumbles, his gaze lowered.

My throat catches. "So am I."

One step forward, two steps back.

Suddenly snowflakes begin to fall from the sky, fluttering all around me. I look up to find heavy, full clouds. I head for the main house, the wet from the snow combining with the tears falling down my face.

I manage to reach the bathroom, grabbing a tissue from a box on the shelf.

Just as I wipe away the last tear, a knock at the door startles me. "Yes?"

"Lily dear, are you all right?"

I blow my nose as quietly as I can. "Yup. Be right out."

I splash cold water on my face, taking a deep breath before opening the door.

Emilia's face falls when she sees me. "Oh no. What did he say now?"

I shake my head. "He didn't say anything. Really. I was just wiping the snow off my face."

Her eyebrows rise in suspicion. "Very well. But speaking of snow, I just got an alert on my phone that we're about to get hit by a blizzard."

My jaw drops. "What? I thought the snow was going to pass over us and hit New England."

"Nope. We're not going to be so lucky. And conditions are going to be treacherous, especially on the road coming up here. Of course you're more than welcome to stay. And it'll make ringing in the New Year so much more fun than all of us spending it separately."

I shake my head. With everything that's happened with Reed, I'd completely lost track of what day it was.

But still, I can't spend the night under the same roof as Grayson and risk doing something stupid in front of him again.

I've already met my daily quota. God knows I'm liable to make more of a fool of myself.

Nope. Not going to happen.

I rush to the closet for my purse and coat. "It's okay, Emilia. I'll be fine. I'll stay longer tomorrow to make up for the work I didn't get to today. I'd better go now if I'm going to get home safely."

I'm already heading for the front door, throwing on my coat as I walk away. "I'll make it," I call to her over my shoulder. "Don't worry about me."

My right hand has just brushed the cold metal of the doorknob when a deep voice rasps behind me, "Don't go."

When I turn I see Grayson staring at me, fists clenched, eyes burning.

"You're going to stay. End of discussion."

A gust of wind pounds the glass in the front windows. The snow is already falling faster and thicker.

Looks like I'm not going anywhere.

"Okay."

* * *

GRAYSON

"Could you open it for me? My hands are kind of tied up at the moment." Lily gestures with her head toward the jar of spaghetti sauce sitting on the counter.

I rise from my seat at the kitchen table and walk over, opening the jar with one swift move and handing it to her.

"Am I your sous-chef now?" I ask.

She grins at me as she dumps the entire contents of the sauce into the pan. "Yup. Looks like it. You okay with that title?"

"Certainly. I think this is the most time I've ever spent in the kitchen."

I watch her in awe as she nods, still smiling while stirring the sauce to mix it with the browned ground beef.

I couldn't believe her: the forecast is for three feet of snow with high winds. How could she possibly have thought of leaving with the threat of such dangerous weather?

Because she wanted to get away from me. Because I'd scared her.

But something in my expression must have eased her worry, because she whispered "Okay," then offered to cook dinner, which completely surprised me. Her kindness left me with a sense of warmth that penetrated my skin, giving me such a high that instead of retreating to my studio, I stayed in the kitchen to be near her.

I followed Lily into the kitchen and watched with a helpless grin as she searched the refrigerator for something to cook for dinner. She came up with a pack of fresh ground beef, a loaf of garlic bread from the freezer, and a box of thin spaghetti and a jar of pasta sauce from the pantry. She did all this while talking to herself in the most beguiling manner. She knew I was in the kitchen, of course, but how she hummed when she searched for the ingredients then gasped with delight when she found them…There was no other place on Earth that I wanted to be at that moment. When I asked her what she was going to make, she replied, "Spagbol," to which I gave her a look of complete confusion. Judging by the light in her eyes, she was amused by my curiosity. "It's short for Spaghetti Bolognese. It was a staple in my house when I was growing up. Still is."

The sound of a glass lid closing over metal jolts me back. "There," she announces. "All done. Now we just have to let it simmer for fifteen minutes."

She reaches for a plastic timer on the counter and sets it, then raises her arms as she stretches her back. I can't help but notice the curves of her body, the outline of her breasts against the fabric of her sweater.

I quickly rise to my feet to shake off the thoughts swirling in my head of what Lily must look like naked. "Wine?" I ask.

"Yes, that would be great, thanks."

I'm relieved she doesn't notice how red my face is or the rising bulge in my jeans. I open the fridge, allowing the cool temperature to calm me. I pull out a chilled bottle of Sauvignon Blanc, along with two glasses from the cabinet, before returning to the table.

Her face is flushed pink from the heat of the stove, and she watches as I pour the wine. With a wide grin, she accepts the glass from me. "Thank you," she says, followed by a contented "Ahhh."

I swiftly sit back down to hide the fact that my pants are growing tented, but then I notice something about her hands as she puts the glass down.

I point to the bare ring finger on her left hand. "You're not wearing your ring."

Lily rubs the spot as if to heal a wound. "Yes. I broke up with Reed," she whispers.

Thank God.

I purse my lips shut at her admission to keep myself from

verbalizing my reaction or grinning like a prizewinner. Not that I have any intentions toward her—as if I could ever deserve her—but from the modicum of information I have about him, I'm relieved to know she's free of him. But then I can't help my curiosity. "What happened? That is, of course, if you don't mind me asking since it's truly none—"

I stop rambling when something warm settles on my left hand. Lily's right hand.

"It's all right. I don't mind. I just realized we weren't meant for each other, that deep down we were just too different. I think I needed him for security. To feel like I belonged somewhere with someone. It was just my mom and me for so long after my father left us that I guess I just clung to the first real thing that offered me affection and comfort."

I nod as she pulls her hand away, already feeling the emptiness of the loss of her touch. "How old were you when your father abandoned you?"

"Five. One day he just decided he didn't want to be married or be a dad anymore. We haven't heard from him since."

"It must've been so difficult for you and your mother."

She sighs. "It was, but my mom is a fighter. She was a stay-at-home mom before he left, and that was all she ever wanted to be. But after he left us she decided to become a nurse, so she took classes while I was at school, and thankfully we have the best neighbors who were always there to babysit me or help out however we needed. My mom got her degree and worked her way up at the hospital, and now she's the head of the ER nurses at the hospital in Hudson."

Lily shrugs her shoulders. "So, that's my story. What about you?"

My eyes pop at her direct question, causing her to cover her mouth with her hand in embarrassment. "Oh God, I'm so sorry. I didn't mean it to come out like that."

"Lily, it's fine."

She sits back slightly in her chair, her face red.

"You mean this?" I ask, pointing to the scar on my face.

She nods silently.

"You know about the accident. When I woke up in the hospital, Emilia told me my parents were dead. My face was wrapped in bandages, and I didn't know why. Then I was told that flying glass caused the scarring. The surgeons did the best they could, but the scars just healed the way they did. After my recovery, I went back to school, but my classmates tormented me constantly, so Emilia pulled me out of there and I was homeschooled from that point on. It's how I got my college degree from Ashby as well. My parents appointed her my legal guardian in their will, and I don't know what I would do without her."

Tears suddenly appear in the corners of Lily's eyes. "I'm so sorry, Grayson."

I sit up straight in my chair. "That's very kind of you, but I don't want your pity. I have my art. That's all I need."

Lily shrinks back in her chair, shutting her eyes. "I was just…never mind."

I watch helplessly as she quickly rises from her chair, the sound of wood scraping against tile echoing in the kitchen.

"The meat sauce should be ready soon," she mutters to herself as she walks away.

I shut my eyes with regret. That's the second time she's tried to be nice to me and I just cut her off.

I get up and slowly approach her. She quietly stirs the sauce, blinking, no doubt, to get rid of the tears.

I gently touch her shoulder. "Lily, I'm sorry."

She jumps at my touch. "It's fine."

The buzz of the timer startles us both. "You should go tell Emilia dinner's ready," she suggests, still not looking at me. "Or if you like you could set the table while I rinse the pasta."

I purse my lips together in frustration. No matter what I do, I always manage to make things worse, causing her pain.

"I'll take care of all that. I also need to get a bottle of champagne from the cellar to be chill before midnight," I tell her.

"Fine," she replies quietly.

I walk away to head upstairs.

* * *

LILY

"That was delicious," Emilia exclaims with a satisfied sigh.

We all lean back in our chairs at the kitchen table, having just consumed homemade hot fudge sundaes, the ingredients for which we found after scrounging through the pantry and cabinets. "By the way, what was in that spaghetti sauce?" she asks.

I place my index finger over my lips. "Shh. Family secret."

A deep, throaty chortle erupts next to me.

Emilia and I both look over at Grayson. "Did you just laugh?" she asks him.

He reaches for the napkin in his lap, wiping his mouth. "Yes. Was I not supposed to?"

"No, it's just…" Emilia seems at a loss for words.

"Geez, that wasn't even one of my good jokes," I offer, helping out Emilia. "I'd love to see what happens when I'm really working the room."

Grayson allows himself a small grin. "Perhaps you will, if you offer something worthy of such a reaction."

I stare at him, tilting my head curiously at first, then nodding in return. "Challenge accepted, Mr. Shaw."

We grin at each other helplessly, but the sound of a chair screeching across tile snaps us back to Emilia. Her voice shakes nervously as she addresses us. "I can't believe it's almost midnight. Let's get out the champagne, shall we? I'll just get the glasses from the dining room."

Grayson and I exchange a confused glance.

"I'll go help her," I tell him and push back from the table, rising hurriedly to my feet before he can reply or stop me.

When I reach Emilia, she is standing at the sideboard holding its edge with both hands.

"The glasses should be in their usual spot," I quietly offer. "I just polished them last week."

"I'm sure they're where they should be," she whispers.

I step closer to her. "Have I done something wrong? Something to offend you? If I have…"

She shakes her head, turning to face me. "No, dear. It's nothing like that."

"I know I've only been working here a short time, but I hope you know you can trust me. You can tell me anything."

Emilia's face softens at my reply. "I was married twice."

"I didn't know that," I answer.

"Thomas Mitchell was the love of my life. He was the boy next door. Literally. Right here in Cottage Grove. After I left my first husband, I moved back home. Thomas was still there living with his parents. He was a groundskeeper here at the estate and he got me a job as a cook. We were in love, but when I found out I couldn't have children I tried to break up with him because I knew he wanted a family. But he wouldn't hear of it, stubborn man. We got married and we were so happy. When Grayson was born, he was like a son to us. Then Thomas had a heart attack, and all I had were the Shaws."

"But what about your own family? It sounds like you're not close with them."

"My parents adored the first man I married because he had money and social status, which was the image my middle-class parents wanted for themselves—their daughter living the idyllic life as the perfect wife to a rich husband. But he was a cruel man who found fault with everything I did. After two years, I knew I couldn't live a life of lies and I left him. My parents let me move back in with them, but they were always quick to voice their disappointment and remind me of the grave mistake I'd made by leaving him."

"Sounds familiar," I mumble to myself.

"Thomas and I had thirty-five years of happiness together. And I want nothing more than Grayson finding that kind of joy for himself."

I swallow. "I can understand that."

Emilia reaches out to me, taking my hands in hers. "Lily, like you said, you haven't been employed here very long, but I can tell that you are a good person with a kind heart. Just from being who you are, you have changed Grayson. He's gradually coming out of the shell he's used as an excuse to hide away from the rest of the world. My worry is that if you leave he'll close himself off for good and never come out again. I mean, he laughed at the table just now. *Laughed.* I can't even recall the last time that's happened."

I notice tears forming in Emilia's eyes. I gently squeeze her hands. "Stop. Please. I'm not going anywhere. I promise. I need this job. And I know how important Grayson is to you—"

"You call him Grayson now," she interrupts.

"Yes."

She rubs her right thumb over the empty ring finger on my left hand. "And I notice you're not wearing your engagement ring anymore."

"Let's just say my former fiancé and your first husband share many common traits."

She nods in understanding. "Then what you did was for the best."

"Yes, but I didn't break with him because of Grayson. I did it for myself, because Reed and I weren't meant to be together."

She pauses a moment. "You do care for Grayson, don't you?"

I pause before I reply, finally addressing the truth that I've been too afraid to accept. "Yes," I whisper.

Emilia smiles warmly as a throat clears loudly behind us.

We turn to find Grayson standing in the doorway, holding a bottle of champagne. "I'm not drinking this by myself, am I?"

Emilia and I shake our heads. "No, you're not," Emilia replies. She drops her hands from mine, walking over to the tall cabinet where the crystal glassware is kept. Wiping her eyes, she carefully pulls out three glasses and hands one to me.

The pop of a champagne cork startles us both. I quickly offer one to Grayson to catch the overflow of liquid erupting from the bottle, followed by the two flutes Emilia is holding.

At that moment, the grandfather clock in the foyer starts to chime.

"Happy New Year!" we exclaim simultaneously, clinking our glasses together.

After taking our sips, Emilia embraces me with a kiss on the cheek, then does the same with Grayson.

And then, it's my turn with Grayson.

He leans down to hug me. I breathe in his clean, masculine scent as his mouth brushes my cheek, his stubble grazing my skin.

"Happy New Year, Lily," he rasps into my ear.

His warm breath tickles my neck. My heartbeat races as I hold tightly onto his arms, the corded veins in his forearms stretching the sleeves of his cuffed shirt.

My throat goes dry, heady from the sensations of his body, his scent, his warmth, his voice. "Happy New Year, Grayson," I manage to reply.

Stepping back from him I take a long sip of champagne, acknowledging Grayson's heated eyes and Emilia's contented grin.

This is too much. I don't…I can't…

My head starts to spin. "I…I should go do the dishes."

Emilia's soft hand lands on my shoulder, and she gently takes my glass from my hand. "Why don't we retire for the evening? It's been a long day. The dishes can wait, my dear. The bed in the blue guest room is all made up for you. Turn right at the top of the stairs. It's the last room on the left."

"Oh, I thought I'd just make up one of the sofas in the living room because I'm not allowed—"

"I trust you, Lily." The determined tone in Grayson's voice shifts my eyes to his face. His jaw is clenched, his gaze narrowed on me.

"Thank you both. Good night."

Sleep. Oh, God. Yes, please.

Chapter Sixteen

"…but I don't want your pity. I have my art. That's all I need."
"Happy New Year, Lily."

Thanks to those words, I slept fitfully in one of the most comfortable beds ever. I should've had a more restful night sleeping on sheets with a thread count that's more than my monthly salary, but because of how Grayson behaved toward me last night, I tossed and turned and barely got a wink.

I wish I could get a read on him. One minute he's so kind and sweet to me, and in the next he shuts down and turns cold and distant. Which is why I'm mopping the kitchen floor the next morning with "Shake It Off" blasting through my ear buds. Taylor Swift just happens to fit my mood perfectly.

Then again, despite his status as a famous artist, Grayson is still a man and it's a truth universally acknowledged that men loathe talking about their feelings.

I sweep the mop across the floor in the foyer to the beat of the song. I pick up the pace, hearing nothing but the lyrics and the music, oblivious to everything around me.

So when someone taps me on my right shoulder, I scream full-throated and jump what feels like a foot into the air, dropping the mop.

When I spin around, Grayson is staring at me with an amused grin on his face. He's dressed casually in pressed jeans, a grey button-down shirt, and suede loafers, as if he were going out some-where, but that couldn't be. "I'm sorry, I didn't mean to scare you."

My heart won't stop racing like a Formula One car, and my hand's over my chest as I try to catch my breath. I yank one of the buds out of my ear. "No worries. I just aged about fifty years. I no-tice you do that a lot, though—surprise me, that is."

Then I stop breathing because I think I just insulted him, but thankfully he smiles at me.

"Is there something you need?" I ask.

A serious look crosses his face. "Yes. I need you to accept my invitation to have lunch with me."

And the surprises just keep coming.

My eyebrows furrow in confusion. I pull my iPod from the pocket of my sweats and shut off Taylor's voice. "I'm sorry. Could you repeat that, please? I still had the music on and I could swear you just asked me to share a meal with you."

"You didn't mishear me, Lily. Lunch is waiting for us in the liv-ing room."

I gasp in realization. "Oh, you were serious."

A frown forms across his face, and his scars elongate with his expression. "Forgive me. I just wanted to thank you for a lovely New Year's Eve, but if you're busy I'll just go."

My heart leaps to my throat. I quickly grab him by the arm. "No, wait. Of course I'll have lunch with you. I'm sorry. This is just…unexpected. Just let me clean up."

When I turn to grab the bucket of dirty water, his arm grips mine. "Don't be silly. You look perfect to me. You must be ravenous since it's nearly noon."

I hadn't even noticed the time, trying to shake off my insecurities about last night with Taylor's help.

Suddenly my mind reverses, recalling what he's just said to me. A million thoughts begin to spin around in my head. I warm all over, my cheeks growing pink from the blush.

I look perfect to him?

"Come," he beckons me, gesturing toward the living room.

I nod silently and walk by his side down the hallway.

When we turn right, my eyes widen at the sight in front of me, and I gasp in awe.

A picnic blanket is laid out on the floor. There are tall candles positioned all around the space, illuminating the room. Bottles of wine and sparkling water stand in ice buckets, while cutlery, plates, and napkins sit in anticipation on opposite sides of the blanket.

I inhale deeply to keep myself from becoming emotional from the beauty of it all.

"Wow. I don't know what to say. This is all so lovely. And how did you get all this done when I was working in the kitchen?"

Grayson clears his throat, a sly grin taking over his lush mouth. "I have my ways. And I thought the dining room would be too formal. Since I can't go outside, I thought I would bring the picnic inside."

"It's perfect," I whisper.

When I look at Grayson, his brown eyes bore into mine, molten with heat. He holds out his hand. "Shall we?"

I smile back at him for all of it—the lunch, his chivalrous gestures.

I place my hand in his open one. "You're a true gentleman, Grayson Shaw."

I can see him swallow deeply before gently steering me to the blanket, making sure I sit down before he does, almost as if he were helping me push in my chair if we were sitting formally at his dining room table.

He settles himself in and pops open the white wine, handing me a glass.

"To a fresh start," he toasts us.

I smile back at him so widely, as if my heart will burst from his words. "A fresh start."

He takes a sip from his glass, putting it down to cut me a slice of Brie, handing me a small plate with the cheese, some crackers, and a handful of green grapes. "Forgive me. I completely forgot to ask if you have any dictary restrictions."

I shake my head. "Don't worry. I eat everything."

He laughs at my confession. "Thank goodness for that." His expression suddenly turns serious. "I was concerned when you left us last night. Are you all right now? Did you get enough rest?"

Barely slept a wink, thanks to you.

I nod. "Yes, I'm fine. Much better, thanks."

Poker face. Poker face.

His eyebrows rise at my reply. "Very well. May I ask you a question?"

"Of course."

"Why is my sculpture on campus so important to you?"

I slowly chew on the grape in my mouth, waiting for it to go down my throat before I answer.

Just tell him. You can trust him.

"It's because of my fiancé, Reed." I catch myself. "Well, I guess I should call him my ex-fiancé now."

"The bastard who bruised your wrist."

I gasp at his memory.

"I saw it," he continues, his voice now low and menacing. "No man should ever do that to you, Lily. Never."

I stay silent.

His dark eyes mirror his voice when I look into them. "The sculpture."

I take a sip of my wine for courage. "I always loved that sculpture when I was an undergrad. It's so sad, yet beautiful at the same time. When Reed and I met at Ashby, he was never like that. It's only been in recent months that he became so frigid and indifferent. He became very ambitious about his job."

"What does he do?"

"He's an adjunct prof of computer science."

"I see. Go on."

"So when he became like that around me, I took Ingrid—"

"Who's Ingrid?"

I laugh. "My car. It's a Volvo. You know. From Sweden?"

An amused grin forms across his face. "Understood."

"I would take Ingrid to campus and just sit in front of *The Lovers*. The way she holds him to her chest. I just found such comfort in them."

Grayson points to my wrist as if the bruise was still there. "And how did that happen?"

"The night we came back from Sunday brunch at his parents' house in Saratoga, we had an argument in the car and I raised my voice. He pulled over and grabbed my wrist and yelled at me not to ever speak to him like that. He was fine after that. But then the fire happened at Ashby and I found out what kind of man he really is, so that was the end of us."

"What do you mean by that?"

I sigh and brace myself. "I was in town when the fire broke out. I drove to campus to make sure he was safe, and I saw him being led out of the art studio, followed by the woman who's the new chair of his department. They were dressed…well, let's just say I could tell they barely had time to get their clothes back on before the firemen got them out."

"You mean they were…"

I nod in reply.

"Bastard," he mutters under his breath. "If he ever—"

I reach out to touch his hand. "Grayson, I'm fine. Really. He's out of my life for good, and I'm totally okay with that."

He glances at my hand on his, then at me. "Where are you living now?"

"With my mom in Catskill."

He nods in relief. "Good."

"I still need to go back and get the rest of my things."

"I wish I could go with you to make sure he won't hurt you," he murmurs.

I reach across the blanket, covering his hand with mine. "I'll make sure he's not there when I go."

"You're always safe with me. I promise, Lily."

I grin back at him. "I know. Now, since I told you about *The Lovers*, it's your turn to tell me why you became a sculptor."

He clears his throat. "After my parents died, Emilia hired various child psychologists to get me through the trauma, but none of them truly helped me. And then she read about art therapy for children. She found someone locally, and since then, art has become my outlet. I was home schooled, and when my therapist taught me the basics of sculpting I found myself and what I was meant to do. Sculpting is my passion."

Grayson shuts his eyes. I take his hand in mine. "You don't have to continue if it's too painful."

He shakes his head. "No, I want to. For painting, you use a brush, but in sculpting, you use your actual hands, your muscles; every part of your body is involved in the process. When I'm creating something I feel alive, and I forget what I look like because I'm creating something beautiful."

I don't say a word. His deep voice forms a cocoon around me, like the warm blanket we're sitting on. I can't fill the void with empty words. It would feel so wrong. I simply grip his hand more tightly.

When he sees our entangled fingers, he continues. "Every time I close my eyes, all I see is you. On the days you're not here, I stand at the window in the bedroom and mentally will your car…Ingrid…to appear in the driveway. You are so beautiful, and I wish I was good enough for you."

Oh my God.

I stare at him so hard as he waits for me to say something, but I can't. Without even realizing I'm doing it, I slowly inch myself closer to him until our knees touch. I carefully reach out my right hand to his face and gently trace his scars with my fingers. His eyes are closed, absorbing every touch.

"You are, Grayson. You are good enough for me," I reassure him. "I just don't think I'm the same for you."

Suddenly his warm brown eyes open. He cups his hand over mine, moving his mouth toward my palm, then the rice paper-thin skin on my wrist where Reed hurt me. He softly kisses me there, sending electric pulses up my arm to the rest of my body.

"Grayson…"

Without warning, he pulls me closer to him, running his thumbs over my cheeks. I can feel the warmth of his breath on my face. He's coming closer and closer with his lips almost taking mine…

"Excuse me?"

We pull back from each other at the sound of Emilia's voice behind me. When we glance over to her, she's waving a letter in her hand. "I'm so sorry, but I think you should see this, Grayson. It actually concerns Lily as well."

He leaps to his feet, brushing crumbs off his pants. "What's happened?" he demands.

My eyes widen at his tone. "I'm sure it's nothing," I offer in an attempt to ease his concern.

"Lily's right," Emilia says. "It's from the president of Ashby College. It's a request for a donation or some kind of aid to help restore the art studio that was destroyed in the fire."

He takes the letter from Emilia, skimming it. "I see. Well, what do you suggest we donate? Maybe they can auction off a piece of mine. We can go through the inventory, see what—"

My mouth opens and words form before I can stop them. "I have an idea. A masquerade ball."

Emilia and Grayson both turn to me with questioning looks on their faces.

"A ball?" Grayson asks, a disgusted look on his face.

Deep breath. Go on.

"Yes. I think it could raise much more money than a simple auction. You could invite the trustees, the faculty. There are also the art lovers in Hudson, the ones who donate money and sponsor benefit events to preserve the Thomas Cole and Frederick Edwin Church houses. All of the people who've moved here from New York City who have enough money to restore a simple farmhouse and flip it for a million dollars. Are you kidding? They'd love it. And everyone loves to dress up. It'll be fun. And I can help with everything."

Grayson and Emilia stare at me silently.

Oh crap…

"I'm so sorry. It wasn't my place to suggest…"

"Let's do it."

Those three words from Grayson stun both Emilia and me. She speaks before I can form a sentence. "Grayson, that's…that's very generous of you. Are you sure?"

"Yes." He steps over to me. "Forgive me, but I need to cut our lunch short. I need to get to the studio, and I think you might have some work to do now."

Was that a glint in his eye?

My heart drops from my throat, light as a feather. I grin back at him. "Umm, yes, I guess I do. It's okay. Go. I'll clean up."

He gives me a slight smile before walking away.

Emilia taps me on the shoulder. "He's right, my dear. Looks like we have some work to do."

We smile at each other, laughing to ourselves as we head for Emilia's office.

***

GRAYSON

I step back, my hands dropping from the sculpture. Taking a few deep breaths, I admire my progress and can't help but smile.

Not quite there yet, but I'm getting there.

A knock at the door shakes me from my reverie.

Emilia stands outside, holding my dinner tray.

"Come in. Please."

I step back to allow her entry. My eyes remain on the sculpture as Emilia puts the tray down.

"Why did you agree, Grayson?"

I turn to her. "Agree to what?"

"You know what. The ball. I couldn't believe my ears when you said, 'Let's do it.' I thought I'd misheard you. You are who you are, so of course I couldn't help—"

"Her."

"Excuse me?"

"Her. I did it for her. To show her I'm human."

When I glance back at Emilia, her lips are pursed together in thought, then she nods. "I understand. All right, Grayson. Have a good night."

The sound of the door shutting echoes throughout the studio.

I look down at my hands, covered in clay. I need to wash. I need…

I need her.

I rush for the bathroom in the studio.

I quickly strip off my clothes, leaving them on the floor, and turn on the water, hot and unforgiving.

The water flows over me, rinsing my body.

I reach with my right hand for my cock.

She was singing something about haters, players, and shaking something off, whatever that means.

But I wasn't really paying attention to the lyrics.

I was more focused on Lily's beautifully formed backside as she shook it back and forth while she was mopping the floor. Her spectacular ass, so small and round, imagining how soft and supple her flesh would feel beneath my fingers.

I stroke myself slowly at first, remembering her genuine awe at the lunch I'd planned for her. I honestly did organize it as a form of gratitude for yesterday, but I never envisioned our lunch ending the way it did.

She just reached out and touched my face, tracing my hideous scars. No hesitation. No fear.

I never thought something like that could happen.

I can only wonder how sweet she'll taste on my tongue.

I start to stroke myself faster, recalling her soft eyes, her gentle touch. The desire in her eyes so visible.

In my mind, her breasts are pressed against my chest, and when she straddles me I will come in my jeans. I would've taken her right there and then if it hadn't been for Emilia's interruption.

No, that's not true. Lily deserves to be treated with respect, not like how her fiancé did, causing her physical harm.

She likes me for who I am. She genuinely cares about me, wants to know about my art, my process. She doesn't need to tell me these things. I can sense it. Her attraction to me is real, as is mine for her.

The thought of her at the ball in a beautiful gown sends my pulse racing. I can't stop pumping my cock with my fist.

She will look beautiful in whatever she decides to wear.

I'm so close…

My grip tightens on my shaft.

She yells out my name in reverence as I come inside her.

I explode, watching as my release streams to the floor, the water from the showerhead cleansing me.

I turn and slam my back against the tiled wall, my heart pounding.

I shut my eyes as her name crosses my lips. "Lily."

Chapter Seventeen

I look ridiculous."

"Are you freakin' kidding me? You look sexy as hell."

I stare at myself in the full-length mirror, my body squeezed into a confection of red and black lace, the corset so tight and pushing my breasts so far up my chest that they seem to almost brush my chin.

"Sky, I look like a madam at a brothel in Tombstone."

We drove almost an hour north to Albany this morning to check out the one costume rental shop within reasonable distance. I've already rejected the Catwoman outfit that Sky suggested, while she in turn gave me a vehement "Hell no!" when I suggested Elizabeth Bennet. And we both vetoed a princess gown—I'm not that young or naïve anymore.

"This is useless," I sigh in exasperation. "What was I thinking, suggesting a masquerade ball?"

"I'd say you had a serious case of verbal diarrhea," Sky replies from behind my back as she releases me, hook by hook, from the bindings of the corset. "And I don't get why your boss agreed to it so quickly. That makes no sense."

I nod into the dressing room mirror. "I know. If I really think about it, maybe Grayson said yes because he could hide his scars if he wore a mask. And maybe I suggested a masquerade ball for that reason alone. I don't know."

Sky remains quiet behind me.

"Hello? Sky? You still there?"

"Grayson, huh?"

I turn around to look at her. "What?"

Sky's face holds a knowing smirk. "You called him Grayson."

"It's his name," I counter. "And he told me to call me that, not 'Mr. Shaw.'"

She raises her eyebrows at me. "Oh, really…"

I shrug her off. "Ugh. Enough. It doesn't mean anything." Unbound from the corset, I reached for my T-shirt, which is lying on a side chair. My jeans are just about zipped when someone knocks on the door.

"How is it going in there?"

Sky opens the dressing room door, finding the bespectacled older woman who helped me earlier, now holding a huge black binder.

"None of these are me," I offer apologetically. "I might as well just stay behind the scenes and help out the catering staff since I can't find anything to wear."

"Oh, shush. I won't hear of it," the older woman says. "Now tell me: what are your favorite books?"

I pause. "Well, my top two are *Pride and Prejudice* and *The Great Gatsby*."

A wide grin appears on the woman's face. She opens the binder excitedly, flipping the laminated pages until she finds what she's looking for. "This!" she exclaims. "This is the one for you."

Sky and I peer into the binder, staring down at the page.

"Yes!" Sky screeches. "You nailed it! Oh my God! And with all of the accessories! Lily, you will look amazing in this!"

Taking in the picture, I imagine myself in the costume.

I nod with a huge smile. "Yes, that's the one."

* * *

GRAYSON

"I look ridiculous."

"You look dashing," Emilia insists.

I stare at myself—dressed in a poet's shirt, vest, pantaloons, boots, a belt with a fake sword and gun strapped to its sides, a kerchief wrapped around my head and tied at the nape of my neck, and an eye patch over my right eye.

"I look like I should be ordering my crew to swab the decks and walk the plank. All I need is a damn parrot perched on my shoulder."

I rip the eye patch off my face, dropping it to the floor. "This is futile. What was I thinking?"

"It's for a good cause, Grayson. You're an alum, for heaven's sake. And…"

"And what?"

"I know you care for Lily more than you like to admit."

I sigh. "What could she possibly see in me?"

Emilia gently cradles my face in her hand. "She sees you, my boy."

I allow myself a slight smile. "Thank you."

"You're quite welcome." She claps her hands together. "Now, I think I have the perfect costume for you."

Emilia pivots back to the clothes, pulling something off the rack I hadn't noticed before.

This time, I smile widely back at her.

My heart begins to beat rapidly as I rise from the bed to take the ensemble from her.

My eyes roam over it, taking it in.

Yes, this is the one. Because I want to look my best for Lily.

Chapter Eighteen

Hello. I'm Lily Moore."

The tall man at the gate, dressed in all black with an earpiece, checks his clipboard. "Good evening, Miss Moore. Go ahead."

My eyes widen like saucers and my jaw drops in awe as I steer Ingrid through the open gates down Grayson's driveway.

The entire drive has been edged with paper lanterns, illuminating the way to the main house.

The beads on my dress jangle with each movement of my arms as I slide into my usual parking spot.

I shut off the engine, checking my face in the rearview mirror one last time, applying one final coat of pale pink lip gloss.

Opening the driver's side door, I exchange my sneakers for the sparkly silver stilettos in the shoebox on the passenger seat.

I gently shove the door shut, not with my usual hip check, so as not to stain the white wool coat that came with my costume rental.

When I make it to the front of the house, I notice the sculpture in the fountain has been cleaned free of dirt and moss, and now gleams from the lights that have been strung around the rim of the basin.

As I walk in a cacophony of noise assaults my ears—guests chatting, music blasting, glasses clinking.

"May I take your coat?"

I look to my right, where a woman in a white shirt with a black tie and pants stands in front of a portable coat rack.

"Yes, thank you."

I hand the woman my coat, taking my coat check number with me.

I slide my mask over my face, walking a few steps into the room to absorb it all. Emilia and I decided to save ourselves the stress of planning the ball ourselves and hired an event planner, who took care of the caterer, wait staff, coat check, and security.

The shine from the newly polished chandeliers almost blinds me. An eight-piece orchestra is playing a 1920s jazz number I recognize, and couples are dancing enthusiastically.

I turn around to check out the dining room. Long tables have been set up to display silver platters of food, both cold and hot. Round tables covered in white damask tablecloths take up the majority of space in the room, and each one has a floral centerpiece with a votive candle.

The beauty of it all overwhelms me.

"They did an amazing job, didn't they?"

Emilia appears to my right in a regal costume—probably Elizabeth I—holding a stick in her right hand with a purple velvet mask attached to the end of it.

"They certainly did, Your Majesty."

She laughs, encircling my shoulders with her left arm. "We were so wise to let someone else do all the hard work so we could enjoy it."

"I was just thinking the same thing. Where is Grayson?"

She shrugs her shoulders. "Who knows. Probably hiding in the studio. He'll come out when he's ready. You should go have something to eat. You look gorgeous, by the way. Straight out of a Fitzgerald novel."

I finger the beads on my knee-length silver dress, then the long string of pearls falling down my chest. I glimpse down at my shimmering silver stockings then nervously adjust the silver head-band holding my blond Clara Bow wig in place. The ends of the bobbed hair tickle my chin.

"Wearing this makes me want to dance the Charleston and drink some bathtub gin," I joke. "It's nice being someone else for a night, though."

Emilia nods. "I agree. And the last time I checked, I think Ashby's art department is going to be very pleased with how much money we've raised."

"That's what matters the most." The smell of roasting food makes my stomach growl. "I think it's time to eat."

Emilia leans over to peck me on the cheek. "Go ahead, my dear. I'll find you if I need anything. Consider yourself off duty tonight."

"Thank you. But find me if you need anything at all."

"Will do."

I watch her disappear into a sea of costumes. I load up a plate with caprese salad, trout almondine, and new potatoes.

Grabbing a glass of champagne from a passing waiter, I sit at an empty table. As I take a bite of the salad, the table starts to vibrate. I check my ringing phone in my clutch, and discover my principal's number on the caller ID.

"Hello, Mr. Palmer. I apologize in advance for the noise. I'm at a party."

"That's quite all right, Lily. And I'm sorry for calling you so late, but I wanted to tell you right away. I'm afraid I'm calling with some bad news."

I hold my left ear closed with my left index finger to shut out the noise. My heart jumps to my throat. "Yes?"

I can barely hear him. "The board has decided against the afterschool program for the ESL students for the spring semester."

My shoulders drop as I begin to shake with anger. "What? They can't do that! The students are going to lose everything they've learned so far."

"I completely understand your frustration. I don't know what our options will be. Maybe we'll hire some teacher aides. But they did offer something that might be of interest to you."

"What is it?" I ask, gritting my teeth to keep myself in check.

"They'd like me to form a summer session for ESL students, like a day camp. It would be in the mornings, and I'd like you to be the head teacher for the younger students."

I gasp. "Oh. I see."

"You don't have to give me an answer right away. Give it some time and call me with your decision when you're ready."

"I will."

"I must go. We'll speak soon. Have a good evening, Lily."

"Thank you, Mr. Palmer. You as well."

I press end on the call, placing my phone on the table, staring at it, trying to make sense of what I've just been told.

Putting the phone back in my clutch, I take a sip of champagne, and pick up my fork to take a bite of my dinner. My mouth is full of trout almondine when I hear someone speak my name.

"Hello, Lily."

Reed is dressed in a pirate costume accentuated by the stupidest looking fake parrot perched on his shoulder and a patch over one of his eyes. He's accompanied by Tabitha, who's wearing the Tombstone madam costume I rejected at the shop in Albany.

You have got to be kidding me.

I purse my lips together to keep myself from bursting into laughter. "Hello, Reed. Dr. Cross." I acknowledge them with a nod.

"Having a good time?" she asks with a smirk.

"Fabulous," I reply a bit too emphatically.

Fuck this shit.

I grab my clutch. "Will you two please excuse me?"

"Lily, I—" Reed starts to address me, but the sound of his voice is lost behind my shoulder.

I need some place to let it all out, away from prying eyes. I head upstairs, unhooking the velvet rope from the stand that cordons off the upper floor. I rush down the hallway for the blue guest bedroom, shutting the door behind me. I start to laugh and laugh, holding my sides to keep them from hurting.

* * *

GRAYSON

I check myself once more pulling down on the sleeves of the tuxedo jacket to make sure they're even.

I place the white mask over my face, and my scars are perfectly hidden.

I'm reaching for the doorknob when I hear someone laughing loudly, nearly to the point of hysteria, in the hallway.

Quickly I open the door and search for the sound, which seems to be coming from a guest bedroom.

I throw the door open to find Lily leaning against the wall, doubled over and holding her sides, laughing openly and freely.

I rush to her, my heart pounding, worried that something's happened.

"Lily!" I shout. "Lily, what's wrong?"

When she finally raises her head, she stops laughing, wiping the corners of her eyes. "Nothing is wrong, Grayson. Nothing at all. I'm just happy and relieved."

What on earth...

"You're not making any sense."

She swallows. "I'm sorry. I didn't mean to scare you."

I step closer to her. "Tell me."

She clears her throat. "I got a call from my school principal that there won't be an afterschool tutoring program for my ESL students, but then he told me there's going to be a summer day camp for them and he wants me to be part of it, which is great. And then right after he called, Reed came up to me with his date, the chair of his department with whom he'd been having an affair."

"The one he was with when the fire broke out?"

"Yup, that's the one."

My fists clench in frustration. "So why were you laughing, Lily? You should be more distraught."

"I'm laughing because she's dressed in a costume that I passed on. She looks like she runs a brothel in some Western and he's in the most ridiculous pirate costume. He even has a fake parrot on his shoulder. I mean, come on!"

I smile to myself. Thank God I went with the tux.

Her blue eyes shimmer in the light. I didn't even take notice of her costume. She's dressed like a '20s flapper; in a silver dress festooned in beads, a blond wig, silver high heels, and a glittery headband, her beauty overwhelming me.

I need to touch her. I reach out to take her hand but I pull back at the last minute.

"How is it downstairs?"

A delighted grin takes over her face. "It's beautiful, Grayson. You should come see for yourself."

"Before I do, I have a question for you."

"Yes?"

"Have you had a chance to dance yet?"

"No," she replies, slightly hesitant.

As if on cue a female voice booms upstairs, launching into the first stanza of "The Nearness of You."

I hold out my hand to her. "May I?"

She nods silently, placing her hand in mine and slowly stepping into my arms.

Lily's head barely reaches my chest, but she's close enough for me to take in the floral perfume she's wearing, intoxicating me.

Heady with sensation, I press her closer to me. Without warning, she lays her head to my chest. I hear her exhale as her body relaxes in my embrace. Her hand grips mine tighter, the one on my shoulder fisting the fabric of my tuxedo jacket.

I glance down at her, her bright blue eyes staring back up at me.

Before I know it's happening, she moves her right hand to my face, gently tracing the edges of my scars with the pads of her fingers.

"Grayson..." she sighs.

My cock grows hard at the tone of her voice saying my name, her eyes so warm and soft, her touch so delicate, caressing my scarred cheek.

"Lily..."

I lean my head closer to hers as she reaches up to me. Our mouths near each other, our lips brushing together. She purses her lips and I panic, thinking she's about to pull back, but instead, she pulls my head down toward hers, grabbing me by the nape of my neck to kiss my lips.

The feel of her lips on mine sends me reeling. With her next kiss, her tongue pokes out slightly, testing me, seeing if I'll respond.

I open my mouth, my tongue grazing hers, quickly becoming entangled as we devour each other. Her warm breath mingles with my own.

I need to hold her closer. My hands move to her backside, hoisting her into my arms. Her legs immediately twine around my waist. I turn around and slam our bodies against the wall to support her. Our shared moans bounce off the high ceilings of the bedroom.

When we finally pull back, our panting breaths are in sync, our gazes are locked with a combination of wonder and surprise. I slowly set her down to the floor. I can sense her legs shaking, but she holds me, tight and steady. Unwavering.

She finds her voice first. "That was…"

I nod. "I know."

"No words."

I touch her face, running my fingers slowly along her reddened cheeks, then her swollen lips.

"You are so beautiful, Lily."

She blushes sweetly.

"Have dinner with me tomorrow night."

Her reply comes swiftly, her joy palpable. "Yes."

I clear my throat. "We should probably go downstairs."

"Probably."

Neither of us moves from the other, not wanting to break the spell of this moment.

Lily pulls me down to her once more, giving me a soft but deep kiss.

I watch her step to the door, giving me one last smile before walking out of the room.

I lean against the wall, my head lolling back.

Did that just happen?

I take in a deep breath, my mind whirring.

I kissed Lily. And she didn't run away.

I inhale again, pushing back from the wall.

I adjust my bow tie.

I give myself one last glance, and I step into the hallway, determined to find Emilia.

I have a dinner to plan.

Chapter Nineteen

Adele is everything.

I decide this as I'm singing loudly off-key in my room. My bed is a mess, piled high with clothes that I just picked up from Reed's house. I thought I would feel bad about leaving, that I would have some sense of loss or sadness.

But I feel none of that because of what happened last night when I saw him with Tabitha, and more importantly, because of the extraordinary kiss between Grayson and me.

Which is why I'm now belting out "Rolling in the Deep" as if I were onstage with Adele herself. I'm cleansing myself of Reed, telling him good-bye and preparing for what I know will be the most amazing night of my life.

"What in the hell?"

I spin around at the sound of my mother's voice. She's dressed in her nurse's uniform, just back from her shift at the hospital. "Hey, Mom."

"You know I love her, but would you kindly turn Adele down?"

I lower the volume on my wireless speakers.

Mom assesses the situation—me singing to my heart's content, the messy bed, the clothes and shoes strewn about the room. "What gives? First, you're breaking up with he-who-shall-remain-nameless, and now, you're just so…"

I end the sentence for her. "Happy."

"Does Grayson Shaw have anything to do with this change in your mood, I ask, already knowing the answer?"

I simply smile at her.

"Ask a stupid question," she mutters. "All right. Tell me everything."

I shrug my shoulders. "Not much to tell. Last night at the ball, Reed showed up with a date, and I was okay with it. Miracle, right? And then…"

"What?" she demands.

"Grayson kissed me and we're having dinner tonight at his house."

"'Not much to tell,' my ass! That is huge, honey. You're positively glowing."

I blush from her compliment, but I know it's time to share more about him with her. "He suffers from agoraphobia, Mom. His parents died when he was five in a horrible car accident. It's how he got these terrible scars on his face."

"Maybe you can help bring him back into the world."

"Take it down a notch, Mom. We just kissed."

She steps over to me to give me a quick hug and a peck on the cheek. "Okay, sweetpea, if you say so. Have fun tonight. Just remember, no glove, no love."

I grimace in reply. "Geez, Mom. I know that."

"Love you, sweetheart," she shouts over her shoulder as she walks out of my bedroom.

"Yeah, yeah, love you too," I yell in return.

I look over at the clock on my nightstand.

Shit. One hour to go.

I pull a dress from the pile on my bed, sliding it over my body.

I check myself in the mirror on my closet door. It hits me that I wore this dress to the last dinner Reed took me to, for my birthday, which seems so long ago.

The doorbell echoes throughout the house.

"Mom? Are you getting it?"

When the bell rings again, I sigh and rush downstairs. Reed is standing on the stoop when I open the door.

His face falls when he sees how I'm dressed. "Hey."

"This isn't a good time, Reed," I tell him as forcefully as I can.

"You have a date?" he asks accusingly.

"It's none of your business."

"Nice, Lily. I came here to ask you to give me another chance, but now I see I wasted my time. Fine with me."

My eyes pop out at him. "Are you kidding me right now? After last night, seeing you with her, you want me back? Give me a break! You cheated on me, Reed. Last time I checked, I don't have the words 'sucker' or 'doormat' tattooed on my forehead."

"Tabitha dumped me."

I pause for a second, then cover my mouth with my hand to keep from laughing in his face. "Are you serious? Well, boo-fucking-hoo. Get out the violins. My heart is breaking for you."

Reed is silent for at least a full minute. He stares at me, a strange look overtaking his face—calm but menacing, his eyes narrowing, his lips pursing together. I stop laughing, tilting my head. "Reed?"

Still no response.

"Reed? I'm sorry, but—"

But then he snaps to attention, as if someone's woken him up. "No, it's fine. Really. I'll see you later."

What the fuck?

I watch, confused, as he heads to his car without looking back at me.

A wave of shivers causes goose bumps to pop up along my arms. I rub them to warm myself.

The feel of the soft material in my hands reminds me of what I was doing before Reed showed up.

I look myself over. I can't help but smile.

Perfect. Grayson will love this.

* * *

GRAYSON

I can't…

Nothing I've ever created with my hands is as beautiful as Lily standing in the doorway of my studio. She's wearing a long-sleeved black jersey dress that accentuates every luscious curve of her body. Black stiletto boots adorn her feet, gilding her sexy form even further.

But what has my cock hardened to the point of pain is her hair. I'm so used to seeing it tied up in a ponytail. This evening, however, it falls freely and cascades past her shoulders. How I want to run it through my fingers and then fist it as I take her…

"Is something wrong?" she asks innocently.

She has no idea how everything is so right at this moment.

Say something, you fool. She'll think something really is wrong.

"You are stunning, Lily. Words just fail me."

A smile of relief lights up her pale face. "Thank you," she whispers, now turning a shade of pink at my compliment.

Her eyes roam over me. "You don't look so bad yourself."

I straighten out the collar on my suit jacket. I dressed up for her. I haven't worn a suit in years, and I worried if it would still fit me. But it did, like a glove.

"My turn to say thank you, then," I reply.

She takes a step toward me. "May I?"

My heart stops when she comes closer. I can smell her now, a cloud of lavender wafting around her.

She reaches up to adjust my tie. "You have no mirrors in the house, Grayson," she offers as an explanation. She pats it down and looks at her handiwork. "There."

I swallow deeply, her scent intoxicating me. "Thank you."

I can't take my eyes from hers. Suddenly a loud growl escapes her stomach.

We both laugh as she blushes. "Well, that wasn't embarrassing."

I offer her my hand. "Let's go feed you."

I take her small hand in mine and lead her into the passageway. I guide her to the dining room, pulling out a chair for her at the table, then pour us each a glass of wine. "I'll be right back."

In the kitchen, I nuke our dinner in the microwave and pull out the salads from the fridge.

As I carry in our dinner on a tray, she begins to rise from her chair. "Do you need any help?"

"Absolutely not. You do enough work around here for me. It's time for me to wait on you."

I serve us both. As we dive into our meal Lily moans, clearly enjoying the food. My cock grow hard at the sound.

I take a long sip of wine. When I glance across at Lily, her eyes are already locked on me. "This is very good, Grayson," she says in a husky tone.

I swallow. "Good…I'm glad you're enjoying it."

With our gazes still on each other, she lifts her glass, her eyes never leaving mine.

"Are you finished?"

She nods silently, and I rise from my seat. "I'll go get dessert."

I can't think of anything but Lily's moans as I pull the chocolate cake Emilia picked up in town from the fridge. I slam the door shut, revealing Lily standing behind it.

I gasp, startled, but when I see Lily's eyes darken, her chest rising and falling so quickly, I don't dare move.

She opens the fridge again, taking the cake from my hands and shutting the door after putting it back inside.

"We'll have that after," she tells me in a deep whisper.

"Lily…"

Without warning she grabs my tie and tugs me close. "I don't know about you, but if I don't kiss you right now—"

I reply by slamming my mouth over hers. I feast on the sensation of her tongue once more in my mouth.

I quickly pull away, just to make sure she's consenting to what I'm hoping will happen in the next few minutes. "Dessert can wait."

"Yes," she moans, her warm breath grazing my face.

I yank her up into my arms just like I did last night. Instantly, she coils her legs around my waist and takes my mouth again.

I turn around, rushing for the staircase. I keep my eyes open to make sure I don't trip carrying such precious cargo, but I still kiss her until I reach the top of the stairs, where I need to catch my breath.

"Please, Grayson," she says, undoubtedly urging me to both reach my bedroom faster and to not stop kissing her.

"Almost there, my beauty," I reassure her.

She is so light in my arms that it takes less than a minute to reach my bedroom. I kick open the door, then push it closed with my back. I place her gently on the floor. My cock turns to granite as she slides down my chest, the soft flesh of her breasts pressing against my body.

I reach out to help her undress, but she stops my hands. "I want to do this for you."

Oh, fuck…

I can't move, watching in awe as Lily reveals herself to me, her eyes never leaving mine except when she pulls her dress over her head. Her lips remain firmly pursed together as she unhooks her bra, one strap…then the other.

My God.

Perfect. Her breasts are beyond anything I could have imagined. So full and round with sweet pink areolas, her nipples pointing straight at me, as if beckoning me to them.

Finally she reaches for her black lace thong to reveal her spectacular bare mound.

I am beyond the point of patience.

"Get on the bed, Lily."

She does as I ask, her legs hanging over the edge. I step toward her and begin to undo her boots. The sound of the first zipper coming undone is the only sound in the room besides our slow exhales. I lean in and kiss each exposed inch of her calf as the zipper reveals more of her leg. I can hear the desire emanating from Lily's throat, so husky and deep.

I do the same with her other boot, letting it fall to the floor. I rise to my feet and begin stripping off my clothes. She sits up, her eyes ablaze as I expose myself to her. I leave my briefs for last, and when I finally remove them my cock juts out like a spring in a clock, no longer confined but now pointing right at Lily.

I see her swallow. I know I'm big, and I'm afraid my size has suddenly put her off.

"I promise I'll be gentle, beauty."

She vehemently shakes her head. "I don't want gentle. I want you to fuck me hard and deep until I forget my own damn name."

I stand stunned, hearing such filthy words coming from her sweet mouth. All of that passion and desire was just hiding beneath the surface, and now I want her to let herself go, to give me every ounce of her, raw and uninhibited. And being the one who gets to experience it makes me the luckiest bastard on the planet.

Lily barely manages to scoot back to the pillows before I jump onto the bed, my body on top of hers, capturing her beneath me.

She instantly wraps her arms around my neck, taking my mouth again. But now, I need more.

I kiss and lick every inch of her, starting with her neck and earlobes, then I trail my tongue down to her breastbone, palming one breast while devouring the other, biting and pulling on her nipple, listening to her throaty groans of pleasure. "Oh, God, yes, Grayson. More. More. Don't fucking stop."

I don't intend to, my beauty.

Now I need to taste her sweetness. I inch my way to the apex between her thighs, making sure she's wet enough for me.

Her pussy is soaked. Her essence is already dripping from her down into the sheet.

I open her outer lips and dive in, not able to hold myself back any longer. I need my mouth on her, to taste her cream on my tongue.

I can't stop licking her. Her screams bounce off the high ceiling in the room, again begging me not to stop. She reaches down and runs her fingers through my hair. I reach out for her with my right arm, and she quickly snatches it and places it over her left breast. I start to twist her nipple, her hand holding me in place, connected as we explore each other, reveling in each other's desires finally becoming a reality.

I shift my head and begin to suck on her clit, using my other hand to stimulate her. I can sense her back arching as her body bucks, her orgasm overtaking her.

I crawl up her body because I want to see her face, what her eyes look like after coming so hard.

She reaches for me and yanks my face to hers, licking her cream off my chin.

"Fuck, baby," I groan. "That is so fucking sexy."

Instead of replying, she kisses me hard again, moaning at the taste of her in my mouth.

She groans in protest when I pull back to grab a condom from my nightstand. When she hears the sound of the packet coming open, she barely manages to speak above a whisper. "Hurry, Grayson."

With shaking hands, I stretch the condom over my cock and settle myself on top of her again. She opens her legs wider for me, and I slowly slide my shaft into her.

Oh, fuck.

She is so tight. So wet…

When I fantasized about finally being inside her, I never imagined the sensation feeling this amazing. I just…fit.

"Fuck me, Grayson," she begs.

I can't hold myself back. I start to thrust myself inside her.

Her voice turns so soft. "Grayson…you feel so fucking good inside me. I never imagined…"

I shut my eyes from the power of her words matching my own thoughts. "You are so fucking amazing, my beauty. I'll never get enough of you."

I can't hold myself back. I pummel her, her ankles now locked around my torso. I hold her down with my hands, our fingers gripping each other so tightly, to the point of pain. I am impervious to it all. I bask in our connection, becoming one with my Lily.

Her muscles clench harder onto my cock. Her cries of ecstasy grow louder. She is so close. I need, I want to hear her shout my name.

"Grayson!"

At her impassioned cry, I start to come hard as she milks my cock, every last drop spilling forth. I can barely keep myself upright, my arms shaking from such exquisite release.

Finally spent, I collapse on top of my beauty, scooping her into my arms, falling to my side.

Neither of us speaks. We just hold onto each other, once lost, now found.

Chapter Twenty

I think we should eat all of our meals this way from now on," Grayson declares.

Sitting naked in his bed as my eyes roam over his exquisite body, I can't argue with that.

"I totally concur with you on that point, Mr. Shaw."

He smiles back at me as he takes a forkful of chocolate cake from his plate. I'm mesmerized, watching his Adam's apple bob up and down as the food slides down his throat. Once I thought him so menacing physically, to the point where he frightened me, but now I find his appearance reassuring, as if nothing bad could happen to me when I'm with him.

"What are your plans for tomorrow?" he asks, taking a sip of the champagne that he brought up with the cake.

"I'm going to sort through my things and get organized. The belongings I brought from Reed's house are still in boxes. I don't know where anything is."

A deep frown extends across his face. "You're sure I can't convince you to stay?"

I laugh at his modest question, brimming with innuendo. "Of course you can try, but I'll still have to leave."

He shrugs his shoulders. "Thought I'd give it a shot."

I lean in to give him a reassuring kiss, enjoying the sweet taste of cocoa and Grayson combined on my tongue. "You can always give it a shot with me, baby."

He pulls me into his lap, running the pads of his fingers gently over my cheeks. "I never thought…" he begins.

I run my hand in return over his scars. "I know. I thought the same. What could you possibly see in me?"

"I see beauty, I see innocence, and I see a spitfire of a woman who doesn't mince words," he says. I smile, nodding at how lovely but true his words are.

"But how could you be attracted to me, being the freak show I am?" he continues.

My heart softens. I wrap one hand around the back of his neck to run my fingers through his silky dark hair while still caressing his face. "I see a beautiful man. I see a good man. I see a man who is talented beyond words. I see someone who wants to be loved but is too afraid of being rejected."

I wait for Grayson to say something but he doesn't, which only spurs me on to make sure he knows something else.

"Don't be afraid, Grayson. I would never reject you. You mean everything to me. You always have, even before I met you. You gave me peace and comfort when I needed it most."

"I will never treat you the way he did."

I lean my forehead to his. "I know you won't."

I glance over at the clock on his mantel. "I hate to do this, but I have to go."

"All right," he whispers with a rasp.

I jump off the bed and begin putting my clothes back on, with Grayson making one last play for my breasts before they disappear behind my bra. I shoo him off, pushing him away while laughing at his attempt.

Taking my hand, he walks me to the door leading to the passageway, turning me to him to give me one last, long, deep kiss. "Call me when you get home."

"I will."

I pause in the doorway, looking over my shoulder.

"What is it, darling?" he asks.

I turn around, biting my bottom lip, wondering if I should address the subject again with him. "Grayson, what would happen if you took one step outside?"

His shaking arm drops my hand. "That's a ridiculous question because it would never happen."

"But haven't you ever wanted to travel and see the rest of the world?"

His face turns red. "No. I'm perfectly fine seeing the world on television or on the Internet."

"But what if there was an emergency and you had to—"

"Lily!"

The fury in his voice stops me, paralyzing me where I stand.

I must be giving off a look of fear in my eyes, because the next thing I know Grayson rushes to me, even though he's less than a foot away, tugging me into his warm embrace. "I'm sorry. I didn't mean to snap at you like that."

I nod. "I know," I reply, muffled in the nook of his chest. "I won't bring it up again. I just wish—" I catch myself. "Never mind. I'll drop it."

I reach up to him on my tiptoes, kissing him briefly but deeply. "I'll see you tomorrow."

He gently pulls my head back to look into my eyes. "Sweet dreams, my beauty."

I walk outside as he gives me one final wave from the doorway before slamming the door shut

As I steer Ingrid carefully along the curving road down the hill to the main road, my mind wanders.

Wouldn't he prefer seeing the Mona Lisa in Paris or the statue of David in Italy up close instead of on a TV screen?

Why doesn't he want to try?

As much as I care for him, can I really see myself with him if he's so restricted by his own fears? We wouldn't be able to go out for a simple meal if we were together. We'd always have to stay inside, hidden away from the world.

A set of headlights suddenly appears behind me, closer than I would like. When I pump the brakes, the car behind mine doesn't back off. Reaching the bottom of the hill, I quickly check the road before peeling out—the car's no longer behind me. I breathe a sigh of relief and turn on the CD player, singing along with Adele at the top of my lungs to calm my nerves.

* * *

GRAYSON

She's right.

What kind of life can I have with Lily if she hides away with me in this cold, aging house?

I can't subject her to that. She is light. She is beauty. She needs to be in the world, not hiding from it. The world needs someone like my Lily in it as an active participant and not me, a creature who would make those who encounter him cringe and run away in horror and disgust.

With my mind spinning, I sit down at the desk in my bedroom and open up my laptop. I type "Agoraphobia—causes and cures" into a search engine, clicking on every link that pops up.

Chapter Twenty-One

Straddling Grayson's lap on the daybed in his studio, I look down to see where we're connected—his huge engorged cock sheathed deeply in my soaked pussy.

He looks down as well. When he brings his eyes back to mine, he takes my face in his hands and kisses me long and deep. "So good," he whispers. "So beautiful."

"Grayson…" is all I can manage in reply. My heart is so heavy when he says something like that to me. He says it with such pure, raw emotion, and I don't say anything for fear of running the moment by blabbering something silly or incoherent.

It's been seven days since we first came together. Seven days since I started having the best sex I've ever had in my life. It doesn't even compare to what I had with Reed. Grayson is so uninhibited, like the beast he is, but he always makes sure that I'm safe and not uncomfortable in any way. I can be myself with him and that makes me feel alive, allowing me to expose parts of myself that I never knew existed.

He leans in and takes one breast into his mouth, devouring it as if it were his last meal. I run my fingers through his hair, arching my back at first to give him complete access, then returning my gaze to him, basking in the sounds he makes as he gives my body his full attention and worship.

He gives the other breast equal attention as I moan in delight. A popping sound echoes through the studio when he releases my breast.

"Ride me, my beauty," he commands.

I start to buck on his strong muscled thighs. He grips my hips to both steady me and angle me so his cock brushes my clit each time they come into contact.

Grayson's hot breath wafts across my face as he grunts, hoisting me up and down. Our eyes lock on each other, our jaws clenched in determination to reach our climax, connecting as one.

I tighten my muscles on his shaft and Grayson instantly increases his speed, his grunts now sounding so primal, arousing me even further.

One more brush of my clit, and my orgasm overtakes me. I buck my hips again and again to milk out every last drop of his cum. His muscles lock under me as he explodes into my pussy.

I collapse onto his chest. His chiseled arms wrap around me, bringing me with him onto the mattress.

"I thought I was coming in here just to ask you what you wanted for dinner, and look what happens."

He laughs into my neck. "I can't help it. I've got a lot of catching up to do."

A question crosses my mind, something that I never thought to ask. "Last week wasn't your first time, was it?"

His eyebrows furrow in concern. "Would that be a problem?"

"Oh, God no," I reassure him. "Of course not. I'm just asking because you definitely knew what you were doing."

"When I was twenty-one, Emilia…erm…hired someone for me."

My eyes widen and my jaw drops in utter shock. "She got you a hooker?"

"No need to be so crass, darling. She was a courtesan."

I roll my eyes at him. "A 'courtesan?' Honey, I hate to break it to you, but courtesans went out with the nineteenth century. That's why you need me as a tour guide in this century."

He huffs in exasperation. "Fine. I'll call her an escort."

I snort at his correction.

"Anyway," he continues, "Emilia did some research, found her on the Internet, and she came over. We had sex, and that was it."

I word my next question gently. "So, that was the only time you did it?"

He nods silently.

I grip him tighter in my embrace. "Well, you won't need to use the Internet ever again since you have me now."

He kisses my forehead. "I know. Lucky me."

"Speaking of that, I think we should talk about my job."

He stiffens in my arms. "What about it?"

"I'm starting to feel awkward taking money from you. I feel like a character in a romance novel. You know, the servant sleeping with the master of the house. I think once the other cleaning woman recovers, I should find another job."

"But you won't leave me, right?"

The fear in his voice shakes me to my core. I sear my eyes into his, running a hand over his scars. "No, Grayson, I'm not leaving you."

He exhales in relief, holding me even closer now as I sigh in his arms, so content.

A thought jolts my body. "Oh, crap, I totally forgot. I brought you something. I left it in my car."

I pry myself from his embrace. "My beauty, it can wait," he says. "It's so cold and dark outside."

I pull on my coat, leaning down to kiss him swiftly on the lips. "I'll be quick."

I head for the studio door, opening it as a gust of cold wind hits me smack in the face. I pull it shut behind me.

I take one step and a gloved hand clamps hard over my mouth. Something cold and sharp presses against my throat.

"Don't make a fucking sound, you slut."

I'd recognize that voice anywhere.

Reed.

"Let me go," I beg him, my voice muffled by his glove.

"Never," he rasps in reply.

He starts to drag me to his car.

This is not happening. I have to let Grayson know.

I bite down on his fingers, causing him to yell in pain.

The door to Grayson's studio flings open. "Lily!"

"Grayson, help me!"

Reed pivots around and starts laughing wickedly at the sight of my wounded beast. "Are you fucking kidding me? You left me for that freak?"

"Fuck you, Reed!" I yell back at him. "Grayson!"

And then I remember…he can't step outside. Not one inch.

"Don't you fucking hurt her!" he snarls back at Reed.

"I'll be fine," I shout calmly to him. "Just go call 911. Reed Shepard. He drives a black BM—"

The sharp metal of the knife now bites into my skin. "Say another word, and I'll kill you right in front of your freak show lover."

My eyes lock with Grayson's to reassure him I'll be okay, but before I can stop him, he rushes outside dressed only in his jeans, immediately falling to the ground.

Reed laughs with menace, holding me in a headlock. "Look at your Quasimodo, Lily. Your freak show trying to protect you. What a fucking loser!"

"Grayson! Listen to my voice!" I shout to him. "Crawl to the door. Don't look anywhere else. Just focus on getting to the door."

"Enough of this shit!" Reed yells, pulling me harder now, to a wooded area on the side of the house where he's parked his car.

He grips my neck while yanking open the door, pushing me in first. He enables the child safety lock so I can't get out.

Turning on the engine, he floors the accelerator and we race for the gate, flying through it.

I look back at the steel gate, still wide open. "How the hell did you open the gate?"

"That security system is a piece of shit."

He drives down the hill, taking every curve at top speed. I hurriedly put on my seat belt.

I look over at him, his eyes fixed on the road ahead. "Reed, please don't do this."

He laughs derisively. "You and I belong together."

Calm. Just stay calm.

"Listen to me. You're not thinking straight. Just pull over, let me drive, and we'll talk this through."

"Like hell we will."

I reach over to grip his arm. "Please, Reed, you're better than this. I know how good you can be."

"You don't know me at all," he growls menacingly.

I tighten my hold on him.

Breathe. One deep breath, in and out…

"Of course I do. You have your good side. I've seen it. But you just have to accept that people change. We've grown apart and we shouldn't be together anymore. I just want you to be happy—"

He takes a curve very fast, and I hold his arm with one hand while the other grabs the edge of the leather seat.

"Reed, please slow down," I plead with him.

"I can't believe you chose that freak over me," he spits out.

"Nothing happened between us until you and I were broken up. Please believe me. It just happened gradually," I beg for him to believe me.

He laughs derisively. "Yeah, right. I don't buy that for a fucking second."

The car gains speed.

"Reed, please slow down."

He shakes my hand off his arm. "Get the hell off—"

Those are the last words I hear before a tree appears straight in our path.

* * *

GRAYSON

"Crawl."

Lily said to crawl to the door.

Save Lily. Save Lily. Save Lily.

My entire body is dead weight. Lifting my right arm, I dig my hand into the cold, wet soil. I grab a fistful, the dirt burrowing under my fingernails.

I reach out with my left arm, doing the same.

I plant my bare feet into the ground. My toes are claws, digging into the grass, giving my useless body leverage so when I—

ROAR! A thunderous sound of raw emotion booms out of my mouth from the deepest recesses of my body. I slide my body along the grass. I gain another few feet closer to the door.

I look up into the open doorway. The lights beckon me to the studio, my sanctuary from the rest of the world. It might as well be a mile instead of a few yards.

Sweat pours into my eyes.

I see Lily's face. I hear her calling out for me.

Save Lily.

I wipe my face against the cool grass, take a deep breath.

One more push…just one more.

I growl as I slide my body once more over the ground. The moisture in the grass helps me along.

I finally reach the doorway, the cold of the tiled floor under my fingertips and my face as I lay myself down.

I exhale a breath in relief. I clench my fists and push myself upright to a sitting position. I breathe in, wiping my brow with the back of my hand.

I reach up for the edge of the table by the door. Using all the strength I have left, I pull myself up.

I reach for the estate phone, jabbing at the numbers.

9.1.1.

A steady female voice answers. "911. What is your emergency?"

I swallow to loosen my dry throat. "A girl...kidnapped. Please save her."

"Sir, who's been kidnapped? When did this happen?"

"It was my...employee. Her ex-fiancé took her from my home at knifepoint."

"I need more details so I can help you, sir."

I nod silently.

Help Lily.

I swallow. "Her name is Lily Moore. She's twenty-four, blond, about five-foot-six. Her boyfriend's name is Reed Shepard. He drives a black BMW. I don't know the license."

"She was taken from your home?"

I hear fingers quickly typing on a keyboard over the phone line. "Yes. I live on Route 19 in Cottage Grove. The Shaw Estate. I'm Grayson Shaw."

"Mr. Shaw, I'm going to send a squad car to you and put out an APB on the BMW."

"Please find her," I beg the anonymous woman before I hang up.

Taking a deep breath, I rush out of the studio into the connecting corridor. I burst through the kitchen door, rushing for Emilia's office. I yank open the file cabinet, searching for the file marked EMPLOYEES.

I find Lily's application, quickly scanning for her emergency contact.

I pick up the phone on Emilia's desk, dialing the numbers, waiting for her to pick up.

The raspy voice of an older woman answers on the other end with audible noise in the background. "This is Joan."

"Mrs. Moore? This is Grayson Shaw. Something's happened to Lily."

A pause. "What? Oh my God! Tell me!" she demands.

"Reed took her. He held a knife to her throat."

"Where is she now?" she shouts.

"I don't know. He left with her. I called the police."

"Oh God…oh God…oh God." Her voice trembles over the line. "Okay, I'll see what I can find out. If she's hurt, they'll bring her here. Please call me if you hear anything."

"I will. I promise. And please…"

"Yes, I'll do the same. I have to go."

The line goes silent on the other end.

So help me if he hurts her in any way….

I dial one last number.

"Grayson, what's wrong?" a sleepy Emilia answers.

"I need you. Lily is in trouble."

"Right. I'm on my way," she replies, now clearly more awake and cognizant.

I hang up and start to pace the kitchen floor. Images of Lily flash through my mind. Her perfectly formed backside swaying back and forth as she mops the floor, me laughing with her, feeling the lush weight of her breasts in my hands just as I'm about to take one succulent nipple into my mouth, the pride in her face when she shows me her portfolio.

After what seems like ages—but is actually twenty minutes—I

hear the front door slam. Emilia rushes into the kitchen, her long winter coat wrapped over her sweat suit and sneakers. She comes straight to me, enveloping me into a tight embrace. "Grayson, are you all right? What happened?"

"We were in the studio. Lily walked into the backyard and her ex-fiancé appeared out of nowhere. He held a knife to her throat and I tried…I couldn't…"

Suddenly, I start to shake. My legs give way as I fall further into Emilia's arms. "I couldn't save her. It's all my fault."

Emilia's arms push me up with all the strength she can muster, leading me backward into one of the kitchen chairs. She eases me down and starts to wipe away my tears.

"Grayson, listen to me. It is not your fault. I know what you suffer from, and there was only so much you could do. Don't blame yourself. Did you call 911?"

"Yes, and Lily's mother. She's a nurse at the hospital."

Emilia nods. "Good." She wipes my hair off my brow. "Right. I'm going to make us some tea. I think we could both use it."

Just as she starts to pour water into the kettle, the house phone rings. I rush for the kitchen extension. "Hello?"

"Mr. Shaw, it's Joan Moore. They just brought in Lily and Reed," she says, her voice calm, her breathing rapid.

"Is she…"

Please let her be alive. Please don't tell me….

"She's alive."

My shoulders drop like boulders with relief. "Thank God. I want to see her, but…"

"Lily's told me about your condition. Is there someone with you?"

"Yes, Emilia. My estate manager."

"Good. If there's any way you can manage it, come to the hospital. Call me before you leave, and I'll meet you in the back of the building. I'll take you to her from there. I have to go."

Mrs. Moore hangs up before I can thank her. I look over at Emilia, her eyes soft and warm.

"How can I do this? I need to be with her, but…."

My eyes look outside the window to the lawn, the trees, the dark…I'm helpless.

"Damn it to hell! Why can't I be normal?"

Without a word, Emilia rushes out of the kitchen to her office. She returns holding a large green hooded jacket.

"This," she exclaims, holding the jacket in her hands out to me. "This is how you'll see Lily."

"I don't understand."

"It's like with horses. You put blinders on them so they won't be distracted with what's around them when they're racing around the track. It belongs to one of the gardeners."

"Emilia, it won't work," I tell her disappointingly.

"Oh, for goodness' sakes, just try it on. If you want to see Lily, this is the only option. And I'll give you some meds I have to keep you calm. But just one pill, so it won't make you loopy."

Lily. Do this for Lily.

Emilia helps me slip into the jacket, throwing the hood over my head. It's at least two sizes too small for my frame, but with the hood on, all I can see is what's in front of me, nothing on the sides.

"What do you think?"

I nod my head. I take a deep breath. "I think this just might work. Get me that pill, Emilia."

Suddenly, a police siren sounds from outside.

Emilia grabs my shoulders. "We'll explain everything to the cops. Then I'll take you to the hospital. Go get the door and I'll find you that pill."

I nod furiously. "Okay."

Lily, I'm coming to you, my beauty.

Chapter Twenty-Two

A soft hand gently caresses my cheek.

"Grayson?"

"No, sweetheart, it's me."

I slowly open my eyes, blinking them a few times to acclimate to the blinding white walls of my hospital room. My throat is dry and scratchy, like sandpaper. I turn my head to the right and my mother's form comes into view.

"Mom."

A single tear falls down her face. "Hi, sweetpea. How do you feel?"

"Like I ran into a tree."

She grimaces in disgust. "Please don't joke. This isn't funny. Are you in any pain?"

I try to sit up, but I can't because every part of my body protests, forcing an "Ow!" out of me. "Get me the Vicodin, Mom. Just leave the bottle by the bed and a full pitcher of water. In fact, give it to me in an IV drip if you can swing it."

"Enough with the jokes. Here." She holds a cup under my mouth with a plastic straw sticking out of it. I slowly swallow the liquid, moaning with every sip as the cool liquid travels down my throat. I nod to tell her I've had enough. Putting the water aside, she shows me how to press a button on some tube that's hooked up to me. Two clicks and suddenly I'm floating.

"Morphine," she offers in explanation.

"Thank God for pharmaceuticals. How bad am I?"

She wipes a stray hair from my forehead. "I raised you right because you put on your seat belt, unlike that shit-for-brains Reed. You're just banged up a bit. The bruises will show up soon. But no internal injuries, thank God."

"What happened to Reed?" I ask hesitantly.

She shakes her head. "He's alive, but only because the airbag saved his ass. He's got a concussion and a broken arm. But I'm tempted to go over there and do some more damage after what he did to my kid. The police arrested him in his bed, according to my staff. I wish I could've seen it."

I start to shiver all over. I glance at the phone on the nightstand. "Mom, can you dial a number for me?"

"Honey, you need to rest."

"I need to hear Grayson's voice. Please."

She nods in understanding. "Okay. What's the number?"

I dictate the number for the main house to her, and she hands me the receiver.

One ring... two rings.

Where could he be?

After several more rings I hand the phone back to Mom. I look away, yawning from the medication.

"It's okay, sweetie. We'll try later," she reassures me.

The sound of a ringing cell phone fills the room. She takes the phone from her pocket and checks the screen. "I should take this."

Mom leans over to kiss my hair, then tucks me in tighter under the scratchy cotton sheet and itchy blanket as I drift off into blissful oblivion.

* * *

GRAYSON

When Emilia pulls up to the rear entrance of the hospital, I spot a petite woman with slightly graying hair in a nurse's uniform standing under the awning.

Emilia parks the car, coming over to my side to help me out. I pull the hood snugly around my head.

"Just look straight ahead," she tells me.

I do as she says, keeping my eyes on the woman.

Once we reach her, she holds out her hand to me, her face warm with no fear in her eyes. "Mr. Shaw, I'm Joan Moore."

"Hello. I wish we were meeting under better circumstances." I turn to Emilia. "This is Emilia, my estate manager."

They exchange greetings, then Mrs. Moore reverts back to me. "Come on. We'll take the service elevator."

We enter the hospital, the antiseptic smell assaulting my nose. Leading us down a long hallway, she presses the call button for the service elevator. I hear it clanking its way down to us, metal on metal.

Finally the elevator stops and opens for us, with Mrs. Moore leading the way. At Lily's floor we take a few turns and finally reach a room with "Moore, Lily" written on the whiteboard outside the door.

Her mother's hand falls on my forearm. "Don't worry. She's by herself. Just be prepared because she's hooked up to machines. She's just had a dose of meds, so she's sleeping now."

I nod. "I understand. Thank you."

"We'll wait here," Emilia says to me.

I take a deep breath and push the door open

I step closer to the bed where Lily is sleeping. Various machines make beeping sounds and a monitor displays her heart rate and blood pressure.

Finally I take in her face, her angelic face, where ugly bruises are already beginning to form.

I seethe in anger, clenching my fists, wishing I could hurt the man who did this to her, but I exhale, calming myself. This isn't what she needs now. What I need.

I sit down in the chair next to her bed. I take her small, warm hand into mine.

"Lily?"

She doesn't respond. I didn't expect her to, but I would give anything to see her glorious blue eyes right now.

"My beauty, I'm here. It's Grayson."

I watch, enraptured, as her chest rises and falls with each breath.

"I'm so sorry I couldn't help you. And I'm just grateful you're here. You're alive."

Words fall out of my mouth, and I can't stop them. I don't want to stop them.

"Maybe it's easier for me to say all this while you're sleeping since you can't talk." I laugh to myself. "You've brought me back to life, Lily. I don't want to lose you now. I never thought someone as beautiful and perfect as you could ever want to be with me. And if you were awake, you'd argue with me and say you're not perfect, but to me, you are. I'm going to be the man you deserve. I'm going to make you very happy, I promise."

I bite my lip to keep myself from breaking down because I'm teetering on the edge and I just have to tell her one more thing, the most important thing of all.

"I love you, Lily Moore."

Chapter Twenty-Three

Easy, sweetheart," my mother urges me as I sit upright to sign my discharge papers.

"I need to get out of here, Mom. I need to see Grayson. I had a dream about him last night and I just…" I look up at her, begging with my eyes. "I need to see him."

I flip my legs over the side of the bed, Mom's hand on my arm to steady me. "Don't worry about Grayson. Let's just get you dressed."

She helps me into a fresh set of sweats that she brought from home, holding me to ensure I don't fall over. I slip my feet into my winter boots, and she adjusts my coat when I put it on.

An orderly enters the room with a wheelchair.

I grimace at the sight. "Oh, come on. I'm perfectly capable of walking out of here on my own two legs."

"Hospital policy, sweetheart," Mom says.

"I thought that was just a medical TV show thing."

"Where do you think they got it from, Miss Smartmouth?"

The orderly laughs to himself.

"Is she like this at work, too?" I ask him.

He simply grins and lies. "No."

"Good answer, young man," Mom says to him in praise.

I'm wheeled out to Mom's Jeep, and the orderly carefully places me in the front seat.

I lean my head against the cool glass of the window as she reverses out of the parking spot, heading for home.

I look out across the Hudson River as we cross over to Catskill. "Mom?"

"Mmm-hmm?"

"Why did you say not to worry about Grayson?"

She doesn't respond until we pull into her driveway.

Turning off the engine, she shifts in her seat to look at me straight on. "He was at the hospital two nights ago."

My heart jumps to my throat. "But...but he couldn't have. He's agoraphobic."

Her eyes soften as she explains. "After Reed took you...that bastard..." she mutters under her breath.

"Go on," I plead with her.

"Grayson called the police, and Emilia brought him over to see you. He refused to leave you, but I insisted he get some rest and I promised to give him frequent updates on your condition."

Only one revelation stands out for me from her account. "He was there? He left his house?"

Mom leans over to touch my cheek. "Yes, sweetheart. He did. For you. He's an exceptional man."

I nod, my throat choking up with unshed tears. "He is."

Silence envelops the interior of the car. I glance over at

Mom, who's looking out the window. I reach for her hand. "What is it?"

She shakes her head before answering. "Sweetpea, are you ready for this?"

"What?"

"From what I saw Grayson is a good man. But he has so many issues. His disfigurement, his agoraphobia. You're signing on for a lot. It's not going to be an easy life for you. Is he truly who you want?"

I clench my fists in frustration. "Mom, I can handle it."

She takes my hand in hers. "Lily, I would never question your ability to handle a delicate situation because you're my kid."

"Damn right." I grin.

"But it's so soon after Reed. Are you sure you don't want to take a break from dating and be on your own for a bit? You know, so you can discover what you really want in a relationship?"

I smile at Mom's concern. "I'm sure. Grayson is who I want to be with. If you could only..."

She reaches over to touch my cheek. "What, honey?"

My eyes start to mist. "If you could only know the way he makes me feel...it's how he sees me like nobody ever has before, or even how I've thought of myself. I can't describe it. I *need* to have that in my life. I *need* him."

Mom's eyes widen at my reply. "Wow. That's so...fucking...romantic."

I burst out laughing. "I know, right?"

Mom suddenly claps her hands together. "Okay, enough of this lovey-dovey crap. Let's get you inside. You need a shower and a proper meal, then I'll drive you over to his house myself."

"Thanks, Mom. But first, I need to hear his voice."

"Okay, honey. I'll bring in your things."

Mom gets out of the car as I reach into my purse, rummaging around for my cell.

I scroll for his number.

After two rings...

"Lily?" his rough, pained voice demands.

"Grayson. I'm here. I'm home."

I hear him exhale deeply. I can hear the smile in his voice. "Thank God."

"I'm so sorry I didn't call before. I was so out of it on the meds, and—"

"You have nothing to apologize for."

"Mom told me that you came to the hospital to see me."

He pauses. "Yes, I did."

"You did that for me."

"I would do anything for you."

"Grayson?"

"Yes, my beauty?"

I swallow as tears form in my eyes. "I love you."

I swear I hear sniffles from his end of the phone. "I love you, too. Come to me."

"Tonight."

"Sooner."

"So bossy."

I hear him laugh out loud before I hit end.

* * *

"Holy crap!" Mom shouts as we drive up to Grayson's house. "This place is huge!"

"Calm down, Mom. It's just a house."

"And all this land. And look at the view of the river from here."

I sigh in exasperation. "Okay, calm down, Mother."

She pulls up to the front door, and my hand's already on the door handle, ready to pop out as soon as she brings the car to a stop.

I peck her quickly on the cheek. "Thanks, Mom."

"Remember, no glove—"

I lean back as I shout in frustration, "Argh! Enough!" I give her a pointed look, then a smile. "Love you."

I walk as quickly as I can to the back of the house because I know he'll be in his studio waiting for me.

Just a few feet from the door, Grayson yanks it open, lifting his hand to me with his palm facing out. "Stop! Don't move!"

I freeze.

I forget to breathe when Grayson takes a step outside, onto the grass. And another. And another.

I can't stop crying or shaking. I keep my hand firmly clamped over my mouth in shock.

Finally he reaches me, folding me gently into his embrace.

"I can't believe it," I cry into his chest. "I'm so proud of you, baby."

"I was so scared. I thought I'd lost you."

"Never. I'm not going anywhere."

I look up at him, smiling so much that my muscles begin to hurt.

"And I have something tell to you," he hints.

"What?"

He grins proudly. "I'm starting therapy to help me get over my agoraphobia. My first session is tomorrow."

I beam at him in return. "That's so wonderful, Grayson."

His dark brown eyes turn into warm chocolate. "I want to be a part of the world again, Lily. And I can't envision myself in it without you by my side. I love you."

I cup his face in my hands, gently running them over his cheeks, taking care with his scars, warming them under my touch. "And I love you."

I squeal with delight and surprise as he picks me up in his arms, carrying me quickly into the studio.

Slamming the door shut with his foot, he kisses me long, hard, and deep. I fist his hair in my hands, returning every kiss with equal passion.

With me still in his arms, Grayson carries me over to the daybed. When he sets me down, his chest rising and falling, his eyes roam over me.

"I want to take all your pain away," he murmurs, so raw and impassioned.

I'm not sure what he means until he slowly starts to help me undress. When he sees the bruises that cover my body from head to toe, his hands clench into tight fists.

I touch his chest. "I'm here, Grayson. I'm okay."

His lips clamp together as he keeps his emotions in check. He nods his head.

I watch as he gently begins to kiss each bruise. He kneels to reach the bruises on my belly, my hips. He turns me around to make sure he doesn't miss any on my back.

When he's satisfied that he got all of them, he stands up and I kiss him slowly. "Thank you," I whisper.

I look on with a full heart as he strips in front of me, laying me down on the bed, taking such care to avoid the bruises when he holds me close.

We lie quietly until Grayson sits up and repositions me on the bed, settling between my thighs.

"Not that I'm going to deny you, my love, but you really don't have to right now," I say.

"Yes, I do," he rumbles. "I need to do this for you. And for me. To claim you as mine."

I lie back on the bed as Grayson wraps his arms around my thighs to hold me in place. The flutter of his lips on my pussy jolts me, and I arch my back and reach down for his hair so I can run my fingers through his silky locks.

"Lily," I hear him groan.

He kisses my outer lips as if he were kissing my mouth, with his warm tongue sucking and licking me deeply. I've never felt such ecstasy before, had someone who adored and worshipped my body the way Grayson does.

He inserts one finger, then two, into me, gently at first, then when he takes my clit into his mouth, his grunts sync with my pleas of "More!" and "Don't stop!"

Finally I reach the cusp, I scream his name, and my release crashes over me. My legs shake, my toes curl, my heart races so fast that I worry it will explode inside my chest.

He inches back up to me, lovingly leaving kisses on my belly, my breasts, my throat.

Finally he reaches my mouth, kissing me slowly and deeply, and I taste myself on his lips.

God, I fucking love that.

When he pulls away, he places his head on my chest, panting heavily.

I slowly run my hand through his hair while trailing the other up and down his back with my fingernails to cool him down

"I'll have to return the favor—" I start to tell him.

He quickly sits up, a serious look crossing his face. "But not until you've recovered and you get your strength back. Understand?"

I can't help but smile, and I kiss him quickly on the lips. "Yes sir."

Grayson lies back down, tucking my body into his as we both drift into blissful sleep.

* * *

GRAYSON

One week later

With a black hoodie firmly pulled over my head, I walk hand in hand with Lily down Main Street in Cottage Grove. I do my best to hide my face, but sometimes the hood slips off and people stare. Thank God for my fierce bodyguard. If someone gives me a second look, Lily simply asks them what they're looking at or jokes about me being *GQ*'s Man of the Year. At first I found it quite rude, but now, I adore her for her protective tendencies.

We're about to walk into the camera shop, where I'm going to insist on buying her a new camera, when she stops suddenly. I am now face to face with Reed Shepard, the vile, hateful bastard who almost took my love away from me.

I can't help but smirk at his appearance. His face is visibly bruised and his arm is covered in a plaster cast, held in place by a sling tied around his neck.

"Lily…I…"

He dares to say her name?

I step in front of her, and she grips my arm so tightly that I can feel her fingers penetrate my coat sleeve.

I sear my eyes into his.

"Grayson, you don't have to," she insists.

"This won't take but a second, darling," I reassure her.

I revert my eyes back to him.

"Listen to me very carefully. You will never speak her name again, you will never approach her again, you will never contact her again. If it weren't for the threat of prison, I would complete what that tree started. You are incredibly lucky to have such rich, devoted parents who can pay off judges and police so you get off with probation. And it's only because of Lily's compassionate heart that she's not pressing charges against you. Such a pathetic excuse for a man, you are. Am I making myself clear, you bastard?"

The pathetic excuse simply nods without saying a word, quickly averting his eyes from Lily and rushing off like a frightened little boy.

Lily turns to me, rips off the hoodie, grabs my face, and kisses me for what seems like ages on a public street.

"My hero," she breathlessly declares when she pulls away. "That was fucking awesome."

Awesome. Another colloquialism I'm adjusting to, but quickly endearing myself to if it means more kisses like that from Lily—and even more than that, more of the look of love and pride in her eyes, the look I intend to live up to for her to have it permanently.

Chapter Twenty-Four

Spring

"One step, one step."

"I swear to God, Grayson, it's enough that you bought me a new camera. But if you got me a new car, I'll kick your ass."

"You love my ass, darling. Why would you want to harm it?"

Sigh.

Insufferable man.

The love of my life is currently leading me blindfolded from the main house to his studio. He's forbidden me from going into his studio for the past two months because he didn't want me to see what he was working on. He even put a sign on the door in huge capital letters:

KEEP OUT! THIS MEANS YOU, MY BEAUTY!

He stops at the door, taking my hand to brush it against the wood. "Feel something?"

I grin. "The sign is missing. You're done?"

"Yes. Just a few more steps."

I hear the door open and sense the cool of the wide space when we walk through together.

"Don't look!" he warns me.

"Whatever," I pout.

"I think we need to get rid of that word from your vocabulary. I find it quite tiresome."

"Fine. Just hurry up, will you, sexy man?"

"Now that term of endearment I think you should keep," I hear him reply from across the room, which means he's standing somewhere near his sculpture.

"Count on it. Are you nearly done?"

Without warning, his hand lands on my shoulder, causing me to jump from surprise. He angles my body in a certain direction, probably so I don't miss anything. "Yes. Ready? One…two…three."

When he unties the scarf, I blink a few times to adjust my eyes, and that's when I see it.

Myself. In hardened clay.

I gasp in shock. "Grayson…"

"What do you think?" he asks, his voice shaky.

I step closer to the sculpture. "May I touch it?"

I look back at him. He nods silently.

My doppelgänger looks straight ahead, a grin encompassing her entire face. She's dressed in a long flowing gown. Her hair cascades down her shoulders. She's holding a bouquet of roses to her chest. She looks so beautiful. So happy.

I can't move and I can't look away.

Grayson comes up behind me and presses his hands to my shoulders.

"Is this how you see me?" I whisper.

He rubs his thumbs across my shoulder blades. "May I confess something to you?"

"Yes."

"I didn't even realize it was you until two months ago. That's why I put the sign on the door. You were always in my head and my heart, and it just carried over into my work."

"I don't know what to say."

"Don't move," he orders as he steps away and pulls off the rest of the tarp from the bottom. I spot his signature, familiar to me as ever, but then I see two words written to the right:

MY BEAUTY

"That's what I'm naming the piece. It's for you, Lily. For my beauty."

I start shaking as I rush to him and yank him into my arms. I can feel his heart pounding against me, his body shivering just as much as mine is. I gulp down the sobs that I can't stop.

"You still didn't tell me if you liked it or not, darling. An artist needs positive reinforcement now and then, you know."

I look up into his brown eyes, soft with emotion.

"I adore it, Grayson."

"Thank God."

His body vibrates with laughter against my own.

I reach up to wipe the moisture from his eyes. "I want to take you somewhere now."

"I'll go anywhere with you, Lily Moore."

"My sanctuary."

* * *

GRAYSON

As much as I love my beauty, she drives like a maniac, which makes me want to obtain my own driver's license as soon as humanly possible.

"It's only because you don't like being driven around by a woman, Mr. Alpha Male."

I shake my head. "Nonsense."

"Yeah, right. Just sit back and enjoy the ride."

And I do. I love seeing the river, the town. I'm slowly coming back to life thanks to Lily's gentle guiding hand.

We pull into the Ashby College visitor parking lot. I cringe at the squeaking sounds of her car doors opening and closing.

I'm definitely buying her a new car. She can protest until she's blue in the face, but I want my beauty safe, in a car built in this century.

We take each other's hands and walk across campus.

I stop a few yards from *The Lovers*. My breath is taken away by the size of it. It's so imposing, yet so personal.

Lily nudges me forward, leading me to a bench nearby.

We don't speak for a few minutes, just to absorb the enormity of this moment.

"When I came here," she whispers, "I used to wonder about you, what you were like. If you were the one who needed that human connection. It was as if I could look into your soul."

I wrap my arm around her shoulders. "It's as if we already knew each other, because when I made this, I felt so alone, and all I wanted was that one connection with another human being who wouldn't run away knowing what I was truly like, both inside and out."

She snuggles into my shoulder. "This actually brought us together. Well, that and a house that needed a decent cleaning."

I lean down and kiss her soft hair. "Indeed."

Suddenly she jumps from the bench, tugging me with her. She walks me closer to the sculpture. "My turn to say 'don't move.'"

"Whatever," I mock in reply.

She begins to search for something in her purse. "I think I've become a bad influence on you."

"Never. What on earth are you looking for?"

"Aha!"

Lily pulls out her cell phone, dropping her purse to the ground. She leans in closer to me. "Lean down."

She turns the phone toward our faces, hits a few buttons, and then we miraculously appear on the screen.

"What are you doing, darling?"

"We're taking our first selfie," she proudly announces.

I do as she asks, then she clicks a button a few times. When she shows me the results, I'm astonished.

"I want that photo on every wall in my house."

"Better yet, we need to get you a smartphone so I can send it to you."

"What kind of phone?"

She takes my face and kisses me sweetly. "Don't worry, Grayson. I'll teach you everything. I'm not going anywhere."

I pull her to me, holding her tight. She instantly wraps her arms around me, settling her head into my chest as I kiss her silky blond hair. "Thank God for that, my beauty."

Chapter Twenty-Five

Summer

I check the clock. Ten minutes to go.

Grayson should be here soon. He likes to meet me after class, then we go out for lunch, take a drive, or do something all regular couples do, something he and I are learning to appreciate as the months go by and we learn more about each other.

My students are working on their ongoing projects—a collage about the favorite parts of their culture. Looking up, I see Ramon biting his lip as he carefully glues a picture to poster board. Olenka is drawing with crayons, and Esperanza's eyebrows narrow as she diligently cuts a picture from a magazine.

A gentle tap on my hand reverts my attention back to Anisa, a new student, who has been practicing writing the alphabet.

Anisa and her twin sister Zahra are new arrivals, refugees from Afghanistan. From what the program director has managed to learn about them, their father was a translator for the US Army who obtained visas for his family after two years of red tape and working through diplomatic channels. Because of their father's occupation, they know some English, but I've also had to teach them basic classroom etiquette, while the other students have shown them social cues, like sharing a snack or holding hands.

I clap my hands five times to gain everyone's attention.

"One, two, three, eyes on me," I shout.

"One, two, eyes on you," the students reply.

I rise from my chair. "Very nice. Boys and girls, please put away your projects in your cubbies and return the supplies to their proper places, then join me on the rug for our cool down activity."

I check Anisa and Zahra's writing. I give them both a big smile. "Very good, girls. You may go join the others," I tell them, pointing to the floor where a few students are already sitting.

I sit down in my chair on the edge of the brightly patterned rug where I lead floor activities with the class. I notice Olenka and Esperanza talking with each other, so I raise my index finger to my lips, waiting until they notice that everyone else is silent.

It certainly helps when Ramon nudges Olenka with his elbow, pressing his finger to his lips, instantly quieting the girls.

"Thank you, boys and girls. What a fun day we have had! Esperanza, who is choosing today's cool down song?"

Her brown eyes dart to the agenda at the front of the room. "Zahra."

I turn to Zahra. "Zahra, what would you like to sing today?"

Her bright green eyes light up. "Itsy Bitsy," she replies, just above a whisper.

"Itsy Bitsy Spider" was the first song we sang altogether on the first day, and it took them a while to learn the hand gestures, but now, both she and Anisa choose it when it's their turn.

"Great choice, Zahra. Let's start…The itsy bitsy spider went up the water spout…"

I smile, watching everyone alternating their thumbs and index fingers, mimicking a climbing spider.

"Down came the rain, and washed the spider out…"

Suddenly, Ramon and Olenka stop singing, dropping their hands. Esperanza points to the door. "Who's that?"

I turn to see Grayson's face in the window of the door, but he just as quickly disappears from view. Usually he waits in the car with Emilia.

"Boys and girls, please stay on the rug. I'll be right back."

I rush to the door, opening it, finding Grayson's walking away. "Grayson, stop! Come back. I can't leave them alone," I plead.

He freezes in place, then pivots around, heading back in my direction.

I hold out my hands to him, which he grasps tightly the instant he reaches me.

"I know I should've waited with Emilia, but I just wanted to see you with the children," he explains, looking down at the floor.

I release his hands to touch his face. "It's totally okay, baby. You can come in if you want. They would love to meet you."

"No," he declines vehemently. "I don't want to scare them."

"You won't, I promise," I reassure him. "And they've already seen you, so the cat's out of the bag." I reply in an attempt at levity.

He nods in agreement.

I take his right hand, leading him back into the classroom.

Ten pairs of eyes immediately zoom in on us. Some mouths open, but the room is silent.

I stand in front of the class, holding the hand of the man I love. "Boys and girls, this is my friend Grayson," I announce to them.

"Hello," he says roughly, clearing his throat.

Some students reply a quiet "Hi," but most of my second graders continue to stare silently.

Grayson's hand grips mine, damp and shaking.

Without warning, Anisa rises from the rug, taking a few steps toward Grayson. She stops in front of him, raising her right arm upward, the fingers on her hand outstretched as if she were reaching for something.

Silent tears form in the corners of my eyes. "Anisa wants to touch your face, honey," I whisper in his ear.

"Oh," he mutters. He clears his throat once more. With his six-foot-three frame towering over Anisa as if he were a giant, he crouches down to her eye level. "Hello, Anisa," he greets her.

She slowly touches Grayson's scars, tracing them with the tiny pads of her fingers. "Hurt?" she asks him quietly.

Grayson slowly shakes his head, placing his massive hand over Anisa's. "No, sweetheart. Not anymore."

She nods with a wide smile as I wipe the corners of my eyes, coughing to rid the lump in my throat.

"Are you Miss Lily's boyfriend?" Ramon boldly asks.

My gaze averts from the tender scene between Grayson and Anisa. "Ramon, that's a very personal question."

"Yes I am," Grayson replies proudly in a loud voice.

I pivot back to Grayson, giving him an angry look as Ramon makes kissing sounds with his mouth.

"Ramon, that's very impolite."

"Good. Her last boyfriend wasn't very nice. But you look nice," Esperanza contributes to the conversation.

"Very nice," Olenka adds.

I roll my eyes and shake my head, looking up the ceiling.

My love life is now a topic of discussion for second graders.

I sound another round of five claps to get the students' attention.

"Boys and girls, the sooner we finish singing the song, the sooner you can go home."

Ramon runs up to Grayson, tugging on his sleeve. "I want him to sit next to me."

Olenka jumps to her feet, and takes his other hand. "No! Me!" she protests.

My heart blooms at the sight of my second graders accepting Grayson without hesitation, no fear whatsoever.

"Why don't we let Grayson decide?" I suggest.

He gives me a grateful look, then looks down at Ramon and Olenka. "Next time, I'll sit next to you, Ramon, but today, I think I know who I would like to sit next to," he declares, walking toward Anisa and Zahra, taking their hands to ease them down onto the rug, one sister on either side of him.

How I love my sexy beast so much at this moment.

We all follow suit, sitting back down on the floor.

"And once more, here we go…" I declare.

My students, my boyfriend, and I launch into the song once more, Grayson following the children's lead, singing right along with everyone else.

My eyes meet Grayson's at the end, his wet from unshed tears.

"Out came the sun and dried up all the rain,
And the itsy bitsy spider climbed up the spout again."
I love you, he mouths at me.
I love you too, I reply, my tears now flowing freely.

Acknowledgments

The fact that you are reading these words is my personal victory. *His Beauty* was supposed to be published two years ago, but then life threw me a huge curveball, plummeting me into a deep, dark ocean from which I thought I'd never be able to come up for air. But with much support and therapy, I'm breathing fresh oxygen once more.

First and foremost, I want to thank the two editors who worked with me on this book, Dana Hamilton in its initial stages and Madeleine Colavita in its final version. I will always be grateful for your patience and support while I tried to figure out how to give Grayson and Lily the story they deserve. Massive thanks to the entire team at Forever Romance/Grand Central Publishing, especially Leah Hultenschmidt, Jodi Rosoff, and the queen of all things for Forever Romance social media, Monisha Lakhotia.

I'd like to give a special shout-out to my acquiring editor Megha Parekh. Megha, I am indebted to you for life for pulling me from the slush pile and taking a chance on me. Working with you on my first four books, you taught me to dig deeper, to push myself, and the true meaning of the author/editor relationship. Thank you, thank you, thank you.

My author friends have been my rock these past two years. Thank you to Katana Collins for her invaluable feedback, K.M. Jackson for sharing Thursday nights in Shondaland with me, Lauren Smith, Kennedy Ryan, Falguni Kothari, Jamie Brenner, Fiona Davis, Keira Montclair; and to the group of lovelies who gave me their counsel and support at RWA in San Diego: Mia Sosa, Lia Riley, Jeanette Grey, Colette Auclair, Rachael Johns, Emily Madden, and Pamela Aares.

I don't know what I would do without my family. I love you so much. Extra tight hugs to my niece and nephew (aka Sweetpea and Lovebug) who never fail to surprise me and teach me what joy truly is.

Dr. Roxanne Partridge—thank you for helping me discover my true self. I look forward to our continued journey together with a healthy mind and an open heart.

All of my friends—you know who you are and what you mean to me. Thank you for being there for me unconditionally, no matter the time or place. Love you, love you, love you!

A special note of appreciation and gratitude to Adele and to Amy Schumer, whose songs and humor, respectively, got me through these past two years.

Finally, to my wonderful readers—this series is very different from my first one, so while you're reading it, I'll be over in the corner breathing into a paper bag. I hope you enjoy Grayson and Lily's story!

Lily and Grayson's story
will conclude in HER BEAST, coming soon.

Chapter One

Autumn

The colors are overwhelming this year. I click away with my Nikon, focusing on the brilliance of the leaves—the reds sharp, the oranges soft, and the yellows shining brightly in the sun.

"Hey! I'm getting cold back here without you," a low, husky male voice calls out behind me.

"Shush! Artist at work!" I shout back to him.

I take a few steps closer to the edge of the lawn.

"If you fall over, I'm not coming to rescue you," he warns me.

"Thanks, babe. I love you too."

A few more clicks and I head back to my boyfriend, Grayson Shaw, who's waiting patiently for me on an outdoor swing that sits on the back end of his family's property, offering a beautiful view of the Catskill Mountains that sit across from us, separated by the Hudson River.

Once I put down my camera he opens the wool blanket

he's wrapped in, allowing me to curl into him as he cocoons us both.

"Kiss, please," he says.

I love how formal he is, always adding "please" when he asks. He's such a gentleman. Well, except when we're having sex. Then the beast comes out, and he never asks...he commands.

I tilt my head up and our lips meet—long, wet, and deep.

Don't miss more great reads from Sofia Tate!

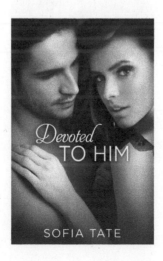

***

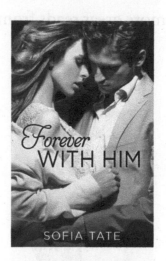

***

About the Author

Growing up in a bilingual family in Maplewood, NJ, Sofia Tate was a shy good girl who attended Catholic school and never misbehaved. Now, she is a proud author of contemporary erotic romance. She graduated from Marymount College in Tarrytown, NY, with a degree in International Studies and a minor in Italian. She also holds an MATESOL from New York University and an MFA in Creative Writing from Adelphi University. She has lived in London and Prague. A former resident of New York City, Sofia currently lives in New York's Hudson Valley

To learn more, visit:

www.sofiatate.com

Twitter: @sofiatateauthor